Ans	_____	M.L.	_____
ASH	_____	MLW	_____
Bev	_____	Mt.Pl	_____
C.C.	_____	NLM	_____
Dick	_____	Ott	_____
DRZ	_____	PC	_____
ECH	_____	PH	_____
ECS	_____	P.P.	_____
Gar	_____	Pion.P.	6/09
GRM	2/10 Hansen	Q.A.	_____
GSP	_____	Riv	_____
G.V.	_____	Ross	_____
Har	_____	S.C.	_____
JPCP	_____	St.A.	_____
KEN	_____	St.J	_____
K.L.	_____	St.Joa	_____
K.M.	_____	St.M.	_____
L.H.	_____	Sgt	_____
LO	_____	T.H.	_____
Lyn	_____	TLLO	_____
L.V.	_____	T.M.	_____
McC	_____	T.T.	_____
McG	_____	Ven	_____
McQ	_____	VP	_____
MIL	_____	Wat	_____
	_____	Wed	_____
	_____	WIL	_____

THE SILVER VINAIGRETTE

After her gambling father leaves her penniless, Phoebe Latimer accepts an invitation to act as companion to semi-invalid Kitty. But she soon realises that the new life she has chosen for herself could be fraught with complications when she encounters Theo Prendergast — Kitty's tyrannical guardian. Even so, she resolves to release Kitty from Theo's claustrophobic protection and indeed finds him overbearing and impossible to deal with . . . yet she is drawn to Theo in a most unsettling manner . . .

BETH JAMES

THE SILVER VINAIGRETTE

Complete and Unabridged

LINFORD
Leicester

First published in Great Britain in 2007

First Linford Edition
published 2009

British Library CIP Data

James, Beth.
   The silver vinaigrette
   1. Love stories.
   2. Large type books.
   I. Title
   823.9'2–dc22

   ISBN 978–1–84782–644–2

Published by
F. A. Thorpe (Publishing)
Anstey, Leicestershire

Set by Words & Graphics Ltd.
Anstey, Leicestershire
Printed and bound in Great Britain by
T. J. International Ltd., Padstow, Cornwall

This book is printed on acid-free paper

1

Phoebe Latimer stood as tall as her diminutive inches would allow and addressed her brother. 'It's no good you climbing on your high horse, Charles, you are not Papa and you never were a match for me, even in the nursery. I cannot and will not marry that disgusting old man, just to please you.'

'Pray don't distress yourself . . . ' said her sister-in-law, Eliza who, at the same time as offering this platitude, wore an expression of supreme smugness on her pretty, but petulant face.

'Never worry — I'm not in the least distressed, and even if I were, it would make no difference. I'd as lief be — I'd rather be a — a kitchen maid before I marry that odious, gout suffering, old man.'

Charles looked down at his sister from under brooding brows. 'I know it

1

ain't entirely to your liking,' he tried again in persuasive tones. 'I wish it could be different, but you know how we are left. Papa's debts have to be paid and we have to keep up a semblance of decency in the manner in which we live. Surely any reasonable offer for you must be considered.'

Phoebe peeled off her evening gloves — made of kid leather in the very height of elegance — with no thought as to their expense. A fire was kindling in her eyes and her mouth took on a stubborn set.

'Reasonable? You call the honourable Sir Henry — nigh on one hundred years old — reasonable? Really Charles, I'd as lief marry a complete down and outer and you know it.'

Looking suitably shocked, Eliza chose to enter the discussion again. 'It's a wonder you receive any offers at all when you show such want of conduct. Have you no respect for your brother?'

The look, which Phoebe cast her, answered the question clear enough.

Charles sighed wearily and lifted a hand to his brow. 'Very well,' he said finally. 'I'll tell Henry your answer, but you would do well to think on your circumstances, Phoebe. Be aware that though he might suffer from the gout, Henry is not much more than forty years and personable enough. You have the whole of your future before you, I need not remind you. You have no dowry, you've been out of the school-room for four years and at one and twenty years, you ain't getting any younger . . . '

With these words, he and Eliza, even whose fair curls were quivering with righteous indignation, left the room and repaired to their bedchamber.

On reaching her own bedchamber, Phoebe's anger left her and after throwing down her gloves and beaded reticule she sank on to her dressing table chair and contemplated her dim looking future. Charles, stuffed shirt though he might be, had a very good point, the outlook did indeed look bleak.

If only Papa hadn't died just when his luck was down. In Phoebe's experience even though her father had often run exceedingly close to the wind, he'd always before managed with a smile and a roguish twinkle in his eye, somehow to come about again. But the unthinkable had happened and although he'd not gone so far as to wager away the whole of his estates, which were entailed to Charles as the eldest son, he'd died with little else to bestow, which meant that Phoebe was indeed left in very straightened circumstances.

Oh, why did she not favour her mother's side of the family whom, with their aristocratic connections were held to be uncommon good looking and good tempered to boot?

Phoebe gave a wry grin at the mirror. Her reflection looked back. Glossy curls, which were alas dark, so very out of fashion at present; eyes that could only be described as commonplace grey, neat features, clear skin, but around the mouth a look of firmness could appear, which Charles was used to call her mulish expression — hardly an attractive attribute.

This expression was very evident now, as unpinning her unfashionably almost ebony-coloured hair from its, none-the-less, modishly upswept style, she brooded on the scene that had just taken place.

But the wrong looks, the wrong personality or not, she would come about. She would contrive a way to leave the stifling atmosphere of depending on Charles and Eliza's charity and living in their house, where she felt as though her only objective in breathing was to find a solvent, suitable, husband.

Resolutely she swallowed down any dreams she'd been foolish enough to entertain in the past. Dreams that involved amusing, handsome suitors who wouldn't give a straw for her penniless state, lack of inches or her pesky temper, and would sweep her off her feet to a charmed life full of love and romance. She knew now that would never happen. But she'd find an escape. She had to.

★ ★ ★

Less than a week later a letter arrived. It was addressed in round, childish writing. But it had been sealed and franked by a person of some standing. Ignoring the enquiring glances cast her way by both Charles and Eliza, Phoebe waited until she reached her room before breaking the seal.

It was from her late mother's goddaughter, Kitty Bellamy. Frowning slightly, Phoebe read the letter to its end, then with a sudden whoop, threw the missive in the air. It was a full two minutes before sobriety set in, and she sat down to read the letter again.

My dear Miss Latimer,

I do not know if you remember me. I only hope to dare that you do because now that some time has passed since I learned that we are both left orphans.

I feel obliged to write you.

Your mother, my godmother, was always used to be so good to me and although I have not set eyes upon you since my dear mother's death, I have fond memories of meeting with you in London, before I was truly out from the schoolroom.

Miss Latimer could and did remember Kitty. Although at the time Kitty, being a full four years her junior besides seeming of a missish and milksop-like disposition, had failed to make a favourable impression on Phoebe. However, that didn't signify because Kitty obviously remembered Phoebe, and in a good light too.

How well I remember your patience in trying to teach me chess, a game for which I fear I have never developed a skill.

A smile pulled at the corners of Phoebe's mouth as she read on. Kitty was sympathetic to Phoebe's loss of a father, she too had lost her father to the Peninsular fever, which being a military man he'd picked up on the Portugese border during the ongoing trouble in Europe.

Kitty had hoped to come to London for the season, but after attending some convivial events last season and becoming ill, it was decided that her constitution was not up to the rigors of socialising at present.

At this point in the letter Phoebe let out an unladylike snort, then just as quickly admonished herself for being less than sympathetic. She was usually aware that her own robust good health was down to good fortune, and was heartily grateful for it. But just at present, when she would so love to be attending the balls and assemblies that were taking place in town, with all the very top of the ton, bound to be present; to read that Kitty had the chance to attend, but was crying off on the grounds of ill health, was hard indeed.

Phoebe read on. Kitty hoped Miss Latimer wouldn't take her sympathy amiss when she said how sorry she was to hear of the new circumstances she was living in. *It is not for want of sensibility that I mention this, only that I would so love to see dear Phoebe again.* In short — Kitty was lonely and searching for a paid companion, and who better, to deal together comfortably, and with whom to do my embroidery, than the daughter of dear late godmother.

At that point Phoebe's frown reappeared between her dark, finely-drawn brows. No, it wouldn't suit. She would be using Kitty's situation just as an escape route. Besides, she'd be no earthly good in a sick room, and as for embroidery? Well — the least said on that subject, the better.

But, oh, it would be so agreeable to get away from Charles' provoking and overbearing ways and Eliza's watching her every mouthful. If only Eliza hadn't brought with her such a large dowry on her marriage to Charles, and if only she had been of a more fun-loving nature, perhaps Phoebe wouldn't have found her close proximity to be so difficult to bear.

It was a crying shame that Kitty had to live in Norfolk. Why could she not reside near Brighton, with its heady mix of social life? Its grand Pavilion built at enormous expense for the Prince Regent; the many balls and assemblies; the private parties; the riding out in modish habit; the admiring glances of the Dandy Set . . . Phoebe sighed.

Even Bath with its gleaming new buildings and the Pump Room where the pick of the ton went to take the waters, would be acceptable. But Norfolk? Damned dull, Papa had said, when asked about Norfolk. Flat landscapes, flat people. For a moment Phoebe missed her father so much that she had difficulty swallowing.

So now, who was being missish?

Phoebe glanced at the letter again. There was no ignoring the wistful entreaty in its tone. Kitty needs some taking out of herself, Phoebe decided.

She needs someone to get rid of the nonsensical notion she's taken into her head that she must be forever sitting doing embroidery. She needs someone to encourage her to go out and about, to enjoy the fresh air, to meet people.

'I'll go,' said Phoebe aloud. 'I'm sure I can like her.'

Convincing Charles would, of course be another matter. The thing to do was to impress upon Eliza just how dull it would be in Norfolk. That Stone Manor was miles from anywhere, although Phoebe knew full well it was moderately close to Norwich. She must tell Charles that she would never consider taking Kitty up on her offer, then gradually allow him to talk her into it.

Capital! If they thought she had taken against it they would be bound to think it would be the very thing. She could almost hear Eliza admonishing Charles how, once she was away from them, Phoebe would become far more appreciative of the way in which they'd shared their Essex home with her these last six months since their father's town house had been sold.

So it was with a nonchalant air that Phoebe later entered the morning room in order to come upon Eliza as though by accident. Eyes gleaming with curiosity, Eliza glanced up from the letter she was writing. Phoebe kept up some inconsequential chatter concerning the purchase of some cambric for the making of a new at home gown, which she sorely needed.

Eliza responded accordingly being much concerned as to its price and serviceability. Presently, when the topic had been exhausted, Eliza turned back towards her writing desk then, as if as an after thought, enquired as to the contents of this morning's missive. 'I do hope this was not in any way bad news, my dear?'

Phoebe shrugged her shoulders. 'Not bad news exactly, no, not at all,' she said in a voice she hoped sounded heavy with boredom. 'It was from Kitty, my mother's god-daughter, as you will recall. She's of a rather vapourish disposition, very young. Not yet eighteen — I do believe. I don't remember her too particularly, other than that she was what I can only describe as a wet goose and a dead bore.'

Eliza's expression changed from one of curiosity to that of a superior being about to deliver her sister-in-law set down. 'Sometimes Phoebe, I'm appalled by your want of sensibility.'

'I daresay,' replied Phoebe. 'But depend upon it, there is nothing either you or Charles can say that will prevail upon me to do as she suggests. I will not be buried alive in the wilds of Norfolk even though she has begged me to go there as her companion.'

'Wait Phoebe,' called Eliza rising from her seat as Phoebe moved purposefully towards the door. 'Only consider . . . Pray do not dismiss this matter out of hand.'

'Eliza, thank you for your concern but my mind is quite made up. It is a nonsensical notion. I should be out of sorts in less than a week. Indeed Kitty would very likely send me packing due to the sensibility that, as you've just pointed out, I am sadly lacking.'

'Fudge,' said Eliza very untypically. 'No-one knows more than I, how exceeding provoking you can be, but if you just thought a little longer before you spoke, well, you could be just the companion to lift an invalid's spirits. I've often remarked upon it to Charles, you have a very cheerful disposition and can be agreeably entertaining when you set your mind to it.'

'Is that so?' answered Phoebe pausing just before leaving the room. 'Well, I'm sure I'd never have thought it. How relieved you must be then, to know of my decision to stay here with you and Charles as the old maid aunt, forever!'

Fortunately her back view was all that Eliza was privy to, so Phoebe's wide grin as she left the room went unnoticed.

★　★　★

Two weeks later found Phoebe rattling around in a post chaise bound for Norwich. Thankfully, she was not usually prone to sickness on long journeys. But, although she would never admit to it, now that she was actually on her way to her new post, it was not only the swaying of the carriage, but trepidation as to the future, that contributed to her digestion feeling a little out of sorts.

However Phoebe did not regret her refusal of Charles' offer of escort to Stone Manor. She had decided to embark on her new independent life as she meant to go on — alone. At the last moment, Charles had taken her to one side, out of earshot of Eliza and thrust a leather pouch into her hands. 'Some extra blunt,' he said gruffly. 'Don't want to see my sister short of a sheet.'

All in all Charles had behaved very properly. Letters had passed back and forth between The Latimers and Theodore Prendergast, Kitty's guardian whom, it became clear, looked after her estate.

It transpired that Kitty, wet goose or not, on attaining the age of five and twenty years or when she married, would come into a considerable fortune. This happy circumstance had the effect of enhancing the notion of Phoebe's proposed position in Eliza's eyes, if no-one else's.

'It seems Kitty's health has always been a sad trial,' said Charles, looking up from a letter he had received from Kitty's guardian. 'Her mama was the same and she died at not much above thirty. Kitty seemed to be gaining in strength however, until the death of her father, which naturally put her back a little, but even so she was considered well enough a year ago to visit London in preparation for the season.'

'How did she do?' asked Phoebe. 'I don't remember mention of her. Usually an heiress receives plenty of remark.'

'That's just it,' continued Charles. 'Poor girl was taken so bad, had to repair to her sick bed. Could scarcely draw breath in the town air. She was sent back to the country where she recovered. But still, to this day, poor Kitty suffers with bouts of giddiness and shortness of breath.'

Phoebe sighed. This was not good news. She had thought that once in Norfolk there might still be some semblance of social life that she could enjoy, but this letter made that notion seem hopeless indeed.

'Charles,' she said on impulse because it was one of the rare occasions when they were alone together. 'Please tell me, if this shouldn't suit — if Kitty doesn't take to me, and you know there's no reason she should because as Eliza says — I don't have a great deal to recommend me — I am not the most patient of sorts. If circumstances make it difficult for me to go on there, might I think to come back — until I set myself to rights, at least?'

Charles looked across at his sister.

'What's this nonsensical notion you've picked up that you have to go? If you don't want to go I shan't make you. Couldn't anyway — you know that. You've always had too much of our father in you for me to boss you about.

'As for Kitty taking a dislike to you — she won't. Never knew anyone who did. Save for Eliza. I don't pretend to know why you two are so pesky with each other, but I can see that it is so,' he looked thoughtful for a moment. 'I daresay Eliza would deal better with you if she were to become a mother herself.'

A wicked smile twitched at the corners of Phoebe's lips. 'Well, the fact that she ain't is at least a blame that you cannot lay at my door!'

For a moment a gleam of amusement showed itself in her brother's eyes. 'You're a saucy piece and one day your tongue will get you into a real hobble . . . '

He broke off and became more serious. 'Sometimes I wonder what's to become of you. You've had your share of suitors setting their caps at you, even with no fortune to your name. But there's no reason for you to go to Norfolk if you ain't of a mind to. Tell me Phoebe, if it really doesn't suit, it is not too late to call it off.'

Phoebe gave herself a mental shake. Everything Charles said was true. She'd had plenty of offers of marriage, but somehow none had appealed. And despite her unruly temper and tendency to become easily bored, she'd always made friends easily and with her vivacity and quickness of wit, cut a dash wherever she went.

There was no reason for her to think she and Kitty wouldn't deal very well together. And it needn't be forever.

It was May now. Summer in the country on a prolonged visit to her mother's god-daughter? What could be more agreeable? Why, after such a long absence, in the autumn she might even prevail upon Charles to set her up for the winter season in London.

'No, I won't cry off. I'll go of course. I'm expected and I can't disappoint Kitty.'

And so it had been decided. Moving now, with the motion of the coach, Phoebe would be looking forward to arriving at Stone Manor, if only life in Norfolk didn't sound so confounded dull.

★   ★   ★

Phoebe was put down at the crossroads on the edge of a village. She stood with her small portmanteau at her feet watching the coach fast disappearing up the main road. Apart from two small boys engaged in kicking a round stone from one side of the street to the other, the village appeared to be deserted.

Well, she hadn't expected a fanfare of trumpets now had she?

She had thought when she'd asked to be put down at Stone Manor that she would turn and see some high gates and perhaps a gatehouse that would be at the entrance of Stone Manor itself. Well, she was mistaken in that at any event.

At that moment a lady of obvious, though somewhat out-moded, gentility came out from a small bakery, on to the street and Phoebe lost no time in hailing her and enquiring as to the whereabouts of Stone Manor.

'This is Stone Manor,' said the lady looking at Phoebe with some curiosity.

'Oh. I was expecting to see a grand house.'

'Ah, you mean Stone Manor?'

Beginning to feel as though a different language was indeed spoken in Norfolk, Phoebe nodded.

The lady pointed in the direction the coach had continued in. 'Stone Manor is not above a mile up the main road, then half a mile up the lane that forks to the left. You should have asked the driver to put you off there.'

Despite knowing that indeed, that was precisely what she had done, Phoebe merely smiled and thanked her.

'We'll show you the way.'

A small freckled face wearing a friendly grin hovered at her elbow. It belonged to one of the two stone-kicking boys. He pulled off his cap. 'I'm Harry and this here is my brother, Tom.' Harry leaned over and snatched the cap from the younger boy's head.

'Hello,' said Tom shyly peeping at her from under a fringe of reddish brown hair.

Phoebe's heart melted. 'Hello Harry, hello Tom,' she said thrusting out a friendly hand. 'It's exceedingly good of you to come to my rescue and show me my way.'

The two boys picked up her portmanteau and Phoebe's protestations died on her lips as she realised they considered it their duty to help her in this manner.

'Do you live near here?' she asked as they progressed in the wake of the coach.

'About another mile further than Stone Manor,' answered the older boy who seemed to do all the talking. 'Are you coming to see Miss Bellamy?'

Phoebe's spirits rose a little. 'Why,

yes she is expecting me, I think. Do you have her acquaintance?'

'Yes,' Tom answered this time. 'We often go there. We like her maze. It's good for hiding in.'

'Yes, I suppose it might be. Is it a big maze?'

'Lord yes,' said Harry. 'It's the largest maze in Norfolk.'

Probably the only maze in Norfolk, thought Phoebe.

'I'll take the other side of that for a little,' she said noticing that Tom was growing red in the face from his exertions in preventing her portmanteau scraping the ground.

It was about an hour past noon and Phoebe was feeling both tired and grubby. Breakfast at her overnight stop in Bury St Edmunds seemed a long way away.

Presently they took a forked turn off the main road. 'This is where the coach should have set you down,' said Harry. 'It's only about half a mile now to the big house.'

The small group straggled their way

down a green dappled lane, which consisted of more twists and turns than Phoebe liked. They were approaching a blind corner now and too late Phoebe heard a thundering of hoofs and the sound of a phaeton carriage being driven at speed.

'Get on the verge,' she shouted to the boys. 'Never mind my baggage.'

Tom clambered on to the grass verge as quick as you like, but Harry was hesitating over leaving the portmanteau in the road. Phoebe flung the baggage to one side and scooping Harry with her, landed in a tangled heap against the hedge opposite.

With a thud of hoofs, and the snorting and shuddering of a pair of well-matched greys, a four-wheeled carriage clattered past and pulled to a stop. The gentleman driver, face black with rage, was struggling to control the horses.

His horsemanship was expert, Phoebe could recognise that, but to drive at such speed on country roads was inexcusable.

Shakily, Phoebe pulled herself to her feet, put an arm round a white-faced Harry and turned to confront the gentleman driver. To her surprise he was looking anything but contrite. On the contrary his expression was one of barely concealed fury.

His mouth though full and sensual was set in a firm line and from under his brooding brows he treated the whole group to a censorious stare, before adjusting his perfectly-fitting top coat, alighting from the phaeton carriage and going to his horses' heads.

'Pray don't trouble yourself over us, sir,' said Phoebe in a voice quivering with rage. 'Never worry that you might have killed one of these boys, who have hardly lived their lives!'

The gentleman turned and treated her to a glare, which must have lasted a full minute.

'You overstate the case. You were none of you, ever in any danger. It was however extremely foolish to be walking with such little care and attention so near to a blind corner. You I suppose, can be forgiven, being no doubt used to townish ways, but you sirs,' he burned both boys with a quelling look, 'you know better.'

'H — How dare you, sir?' Phoebe stuttered with indignation. 'Tear into me if you will, but these boys have been nothing if not gentlemanly in their behaviour towards me ever since I met them . . . '

'Is that indeed so?'

From the corner of her eye Phoebe was aware that Tom, who had scrambled over to stand near his brother, was now shaking visibly and Harry as white faced as ever, was standing as though to attention.

'Indeed it is so,' went on Phoebe. 'What right do you have to admonish these boys? They have treated me with nothing but civility, which is more than can be said for you, for all your fine clothes and slap-up equipage.'

The silence, which followed was deathly. Then Harry said, so quietly Phoebe hardly heard it. 'That's torn it.'

The gentleman's eyes narrowed, and for a moment Phoebe fancied she saw the side of his mouth twitch with either humour or annoyance. 'I have every right,' he said in icy tones. 'Allow me to introduce myself — Theodore Prendergast. My sons I see, have already made your acquaintance.'

Phoebe could think of nothing to say, only how glad she was that neither Eliza nor Charles were there to witness her discomfort as Mr Prendergast retrieved her portmanteau from the hedge, and obliged her to get into the carriage and he would take her to Stone Manor.

'I will do no such thing. As you see I am quite unharmed and can surely walk the last half mile.'

'I don't doubt it,' he said grimly as he turned the horses. 'But I have neither the time nor the patience to put up with any argument. If you don't get in within a minute you will force me to lift you in myself and I am persuaded you would find that excessively uncomfortable, would you not?'

Stiffly Phoebe climbed into the carriage.

'What about your sons?' she asked as he climbed up and took the reigns.

'I don't need you Miss Latimer, to remind me of my sons. However they seem none the worse, for their little adventure. The walk home will do them good. I might turn and pick them up again after I have delivered you safely to Miss Bellamy.'

Phoebe's eyes opened wide. 'You know who I am?'

'Of course,' returned Mr Prendergast coolly. 'Phoebe Latimer. We were expecting you. The post chaise was late and Kitty had the fidgets when you didn't arrive. But we had the notion that maybe you had been set off at the village of Stone Manor, not at Stone Manor itself. Was that not the case?'

Phoebe agreed that yes, it was. Then racked her brains for what say next to the arrogant and intimidating Theo Prendergast.

2

My dear Charles — wrote Phoebe, *As I write this, on my third day at Stone Manor, I trust this letter will find both you and Eliza well.*

I am quite recovered from my journey and find myself comfortable and settled. Kitty though delicate, seems well and has a sweet disposition. Stone Manor is a very great house situated in open parklands with a formal garden and — a maze! There are a large number of servants here. Only think — I have a maid to myself again as I was used to, to help me with my hair and dress.

Kitty, besides having Annie, who was used to be her nurse, continually fussing round her, also has an abigail to help her with her toilet. There is a veritable army of servants here, more even than we was used to when we were children.

A drawing instructor — Richard

Steel, and a singing master — Daniel Benton, both young men of good address, call to instruct Kitty twice a week. She has begged me to join in these lessons although, as you are no doubt thinking Charles, she is likely to change her mind once she hears my voice!

The home Kitty has here is lovely indeed. Eliza would swoon to see the many fashionable pieces here and the pianoforte, which has exceptional tone. Fortunately my playing of the instrument is enough to pass muster, and so make up for my sad lack of tuneful voice.

Phoebe moved her candle closer to her, pushed the filled sheet of parchment to one side of the elegant writing table situated in the corner of her room, and took a new sheet.

It distresses me to inform you, however, that Kitty's guardian, Theo Prendergast, is by far the most detestable man I have ever met in my life! He is not the gentleman-like person we believed him to be. Kitty is in great fear of him, so are all the servants and his two boys of whom I have grown exceeding fond in our few short days of acquaintance.

To be sure, he insists that life is to be made comfortable in every way for Kitty, making it quite a gilded cage she lives in — but it is a prison never the less. It is unfortunate that Kitty has been so encouraged to believe herself an invalid when I am persuaded she is not. Annie, her old nurse, fusses over her constantly, and Kitty will not move above two paces without being reassured that her favourite vinaigrette is safe in her reticule beside her.

Understandable maybe, as it was used to belong to her mother and has a beautiful embossed silver mount. I would very much like it if only it were for carrying scent not smelling salts, which smell exceeding putrid — to my nose at least.

Mr Prendergast is a brute! At our first meeting he drove his phaeton straight at his two sons and me as

31

though we were of no account! Although he drives to an inch and possesses the most splendid pair of matched greys you have ever set eyes on Charles, it was a close run thing he did not kill us all! Then, if you please — he ordered me to get into his carriage, in a manner so high handed it fairly made my blood boil.

When I would do no such thing he advanced upon me in such a threatening manner, a female of Eliza's sensibility would I fear, have fainted from shock. He is a dark brooding man with fiery eyes and a haughty disposition. Although I have to admit his bearing is impressive and his manner to Kitty quite proper and gentle, I do not care for him at all.

After blotting the parchment, Phoebe read through what she had written by the flickering light of her candle. She frowned. Somehow the second page did not convey what she wanted to say at all.

Did she want Charles to arrive here

post haste to take her back to Essex, where Eliza would no doubt rate her for casting a poor first impression and ruining her chances for a new life of independence?

Phoebe sighed. It wouldn't do, she had too much pride to go crawling back to Essex, just because the life here in Norfolk wasn't as she had expected. She signed the first page then held the thick cartridge of the second, to the flame of the candle and watched the paper burn, blacken and wither.

The day-to-day management of Stone Manor moved on oiled wheels. The staff all appeared to be old retainers or related to old retainers and Kitty's welfare seemed uppermost in even the most lowly kitchen maid's mind.

After only a very few days of Kitty's acquaintance, Phoebe understood why. Kitty was delightful. Despite often being short of breath, she never complained and her face would flush with pleasure whenever Phoebe entered the room.

Of Mr Prendergast, Phoebe had only caught the occasional glimpse. She knew from Kitty that he usually rode over two or three times a week, thus combining his love for riding with his need to oversee the running of Kitty's estate.

'Why does he need to do that?' queried Phoebe carelessly. 'I mean you have an estate manager, do you not? I'm very sure my father did not consult his estate manager every whip stitch.'

She broke off, the thought having suddenly struck her that if in fact Papa had consulted his estate manager a little more and the gaming table a little less she would not be in such financial straits.

Kitty's eyes had widened. She was clearly astounded that someone should question any action of Theo's. 'Well yes, but Mr Prendergast you know, was a particular favourite of Father's, who used to be a playmate to his father when they were boys. It's only natural that he should look after my interests and involve himself in my affairs. He is my guardian after all.'

Phoebe opened her mouth to argue that two or three visits a week seemed somewhat excessive then, picturing Eliza's censorious expression at such want of conduct, closed it again.

The good thing was the stern, but thankfully elusive Mr Prendergast often brought his boys with him if he were travelling by phaeton and Phoebe very soon became their firm friend.

During the first week, she was introduced to the best places for newting, and ratting; the tallest tree in the whole of Norfolk, the deepest part of the canal, and the cottage where it was rumoured that a real live witch lived.

Phoebe pronounced herself suitably impressed by all these things and then allowed them to lose her in the maze — which they regarded as their very own territory — then subsequently, to rescue her.

'What d'you think of our maze now?' asked Tom seriously.

'I consider it a-maze-ing,' replied Phoebe equally solemn faced.

'Oh it's a joke,' pronounced Tom after a little thought.

'Actually, it's a pun,' corrected Harry. 'Father does puns. His are capital!'

Was there anything, Phoebe wondered, that the talented Mr Prendergast could not do?

By the end of the second week however, despite any previous misgivings concerning Kitty's guardian, Phoebe convinced herself her dealings with him would be minimal and therefore the future even if sadly lacking in adventure, looked agreeable at least.

Over the last few days Phoebe thought she had detected an improvement in Kitty's health. There was the beginning of a healthy flush in her usually pallid cheeks, and at Phoebe's suggestion, her lacklustre fair hair had been dressed in a more attractive style.

But even so, this morning it soon became apparent that Mrs Manningtree, the housekeeper, and Annie,

Kitty's old nurse, both felt that because her colour was a little high, Kitty shouldn't venture out with Phoebe for a walk in the grounds.

Phoebe bit her lip; she'd never heard such nonsense. 'Well I hope you won't object if I take a stroll out myself. I recall we have a drawing lesson this afternoon and if I'm to stay closed in all day I will have the fidgets and be quite disagreeable company for you.'

Kitty immediately begged Phoebe to go out by all means, and said she only wished her own health was such that she could join her.

'Well, I can't see how it would do the least harm,' offered Phoebe. 'The weather is beautiful and we needn't go far from the house. You could accompany me as far as the sheltered arbour and sit there in the sun while I take a turn or two.'

Kitty raised a pair of anxious blue eyes to hers. 'Oh, do you indeed think so? But what would Annie say?'

Phoebe bit back the retort that

immediately sprung to mind. 'Nothing, if we don't tell her. She isn't your jailer you know! I'll fetch our shawls — although the sunshine outside hardly warrants it.'

For a moment Kitty looked wildly excited at the thought of such disobedience, then a shadow fell across her face.

'Now don't go faint hearted on me,' said Phoebe quickly. 'It's only a walk. You know how you have come to enjoy our walks. It will do you the world of good.'

A few moments later the two girls were walking together in the well laid out gardens and Kitty began chattering with less reserve then Phoebe had seen in her before.

'Why are you so much in awe of Mr Prendergast?' asked Phoebe when Kitty nervously mentioned that Theo might not like it if she were to go on a trip to Norwich or indeed any expedition without first consulting him.

'I don't know precisely,' Kitty confided, 'for he is always, above all things, kind to me in his way. Although he does not easily show affection since his wife, Isabel, died. And now he always looks so stern and never smiles.'

'Yes, I'd noticed.'

'And as well, it's not that I actually think that he would punish me for not doing as I'm bid precisely. It's just that it feels such a presumption, for me to take up so much of his time, him being my guardian — but no blood relation exactly, you understand — I must try to make my demands on his time as few as possible. So I try to be good and not provoke him.'

Phoebe listened to this sincere speech and found her heart softening still more towards Kitty. 'Of course you do,' she said warmly. 'But don't be too concerned about Mr Prendergast. I'm very sure he puts his own feelings first in almost all instances.'

At this Kitty grew quite distressed. 'No, please don't think so. Mr Prendergast has always, always done everything right and proper for me, and wishes only for me to be comfortable. Just look at how he arranged for both Mr Steel and Mr Benton.'

Kitty's face flushed a little at the mention of Mr Benton, Phoebe noticed not for the first time. 'He arranged for them to instruct me when he found how I loved to draw and how my breathing could be helped with the singing. But he can, when he is a little out of humour, I agree, seem forbidding. And I must confess since you've been here he has hardly spent the time with us I expected.'

Despite herself, Phoebe was curious. 'Why should he want to do that?' she asked. 'I formed the opinion that nothing would bore him more than having to spend time with someone of my townish ways.'

'Oh no, I do assure you, you are mistaken. Mr Prendergast is very a-la-mode. He makes several trips to London in a year and usually has a thirst for knowledge about town affairs.'

Phoebe's brows rose. 'Really, I must

confess myself to be surprised.' Although Phoebe was tempted to elaborate a good deal further on her opinion of Mr Prendergast's high handed, superior ways, she held her tongue and instead pointed out a rose that had just unfolded and bent her head to drink in its perfume.

After they've been outside for half an hour, Kitty suggested she should return to the house incase anyone became anxious.

Phoebe laughed. 'Why should you give a fig if they are?' she asked. 'Besides if they care to look out of the back windows they are sure to see us. It's strikes me you're surrounded by old fogies here and could do with more stimulation in your life.'

'That's exactly what Mr Prendergast said when we heard of your plight.'

Phoebe stopped walking so suddenly, that Kitty, who was holding her arm, nearly missed her footing. 'My plight, Kitty?' repeated Phoebe with raised brows.

'Oh forgive me. I would not for the world upset you . . . I did not mean, that I am sorry for you or anything like that — I know you would dislike that excessively, being the sort of person you are. That was why I asked Mr Prendergast to assist me with the letter.'

Phoebe stood as though turned to stone. How dare he discuss her 'plight' with Kitty? How dare he offer her charity under the guise of a direct entreaty to her to be a companion to Kitty?

'Miss Kitty, Miss Kitty.'

Phoebe looked round and saw old Annie, running towards them as though at the very least, the house were on fire.

'Oh dear,' Kitty said. 'I have upset Annie too.'

Phoebe swallowed back some angry tears. 'No you haven't you goose — and you haven't upset me either. But I can see you are fretting so go with Annie back to the house. I'll just walk on to the stables, if you wouldn't mind and I'll come and find you later.'

Before Annie could catch up with them and bestow any reproachful glances her way, Phoebe set off at a brisk pace in the direction of the stables where she would seek solace. Ever since her arrival at Stone Manor she had visited the stables as often as time would allow. She inherited her love of horses from her father, but since her own mount had been sold, had only been able to exercise Eliza's stolid mare on odd occasions, which had all proved confoundedly flat.

Still seething at the thought of Theo Prendergast daring to feel sorry for her, Phoebe's pace didn't slacken as she rounded the corner of the stable block. Suddenly, half her breath was knocked out of her body as she cannoned into a tall male figure coming with equal speed from the opposite direction.

She found herself confronting a row of waistcoat buttons topped by a white stock. A pair of strong hands steadied her shoulders. Phoebe stared at the polished boots inches from her own feet and couldn't stop the blush from spreading to her cheeks.

'I'm s-so sorry,' she stammered and nerved herself to look up.

'The fault was all mine.'

The thin, pale but attractive face of Daniel Benton gazed down at her. Phoebe felt a shudder of relief. 'Oh good morning to you, Mr Benton. I'm so sorry, I didn't expect to see you here.'

The music teacher's serious face broke into a smile. 'It is I who should apologise for startling you.' He glanced down at his coat, brushed at what looked like cats' hairs clinging to his sleeve and a tide of colour washed over his own pale features. 'Forgive me, I must go,' he said abruptly.

Phoebe was only too pleased to let him go. How ridiculous she was to have turned herself into a simpering miss imagining that it was Mr Prendergast who'd held her in a firm and powerful grasp. No, she was very happy that it had been only Daniel Benton covered with boyish confusion at that, not the stern and forbidding Mr Prendergast.

Pausing only for a moment in which she puzzled why it was she'd thought Kitty's drawing lesson was today and the singing not till the morrow, Phoebe shrugged as she watched him go towards the house.

One of the stable cats wound itself round her ankles and she followed it into the yard. With a sigh of pleasure, Phoebe looked round at the well kept stables and patted a dappled head that was nosing over one of the doors. The working atmosphere of the stables never failed to have a soothing effect on her.

A moment later a groom came running to ask her if she required a mount.

'Nothing I'd find more agreeable,' she said more acutely aware than ever of her new station in life. 'But I'd need permission first.' And you're too proud to ask, she thought to herself.

The groom, sensing her mood moved off, leaving Phoebe to pet the horse and brood yet again on how she hated the position she found herself in and how very much she disliked being beholden to a person like Theo Prendergast.

In the background she was aware of male voices discussing a strain on one of the horse's back legs and for a moment she closed her eyes imagining herself back in her father's stable about to go out on a wild ride with him.

'Good morning, Miss Latimer. You need to watch out for George there, he's only sweet tempered if you have a carrot to give him.'

Phoebe's eyes flew open. 'Nonsense,' she said before she could stop herself. 'We've made friends on many an occasion, and I'm persuaded he's a gentle creature.'

Theo was in his riding dress, which fitted him to an inch. His hessian boots were highly polished and his cravat neatly arranged. He was, Phoebe admitted to herself, a fine figure of a man. For a moment they stood contemplating one another, neither of them smiling.

'Used to riding are you?'

Phoebe nodded. 'I like it above all things.'

Mr Prendergast contemplated his boots for a moment. 'Like to take a ride out with me? You can have George here.'

Phoebe's eyes glowed. 'I would indeed.'

'You have a riding habit?'

'Yes, it was in the trunk sent from home.'

Theo's nod was dismissive. 'I should have finished my business here by the time you've changed. I'll have George saddled up and ready. We'll see how you do.'

3

Phoebe was already on her way, running out of the stables then, barely stopping for breath hurrying back through the gardens and up to her room to change. How she longed to be on the back of a horse and galloping, galloping, across green meadows, through woods and copses, out in the fresh air — in the real world. Even the fact that she would have a companion, and who that companion would be, couldn't spoil her feeling of exhilaration.

'You are used to riding,' said Theo some hour later when, after a fast canter across fields and a brisk trot along the side of a canal, they had reined their horses in and were slowly returning to Stone Manor.

Phoebe nodded. 'Was. Yes. My father kept a string of real goers besides the carriage horses, but as you no doubt know, they were all sold at Tattershall's shortly after his death.'

Mr Prendergast offered no sympathy, but after a small silence said that he would consider it a favour if she were to exercise his chestnut mare, as she'd been too long without a good rider.

Phoebe's chin lifted — she wanted no more charity. 'I am surprised sir, you keep a horse you cannot use?'

'I bought her last year intending her for Kitty, but she's rather more high spirited than I fancied and besides, that was when Kitty's health was more robust.' He paused for a moment then gave a thin smile. 'Of course, Harry fancies himself a great rider but he ain't quite up to scratch for the chestnut. I've since purchased George, I think he might do for Kitty when her health improves.'

'And am I to be allowed to ride the chestnut alone? Am I truly trusted enough?' Demurely, Phoebe looked up at him through her lashes.

Still Theo didn't smile. 'You're a

minx,' he said softly. 'And if you are fishing for a compliment on your riding, I'll admit you to be a dab hand. I collect your father was known as a nonesuch in his day, obviously he taught you your riding skills. I am persuaded you would be quite comfortable riding alone. However, I'd advise you to take a groom with you until you are used to the terrain.'

Phoebe nodded, then lent forward to pat George's neck. 'I suppose I was to expect a comment of that nature.'

Theo glanced at her quizzically. 'Now how have I offended you?' he asked quietly.

'Oh, you haven't offended me precisely. That's just the kind of comment I would expect any gentleman to make.'

Mr Prendergast continued to look puzzled.

Phoebe stuck out her chin. 'You haven't the least understanding of what it may be like to be a woman.'

This time a smile did twitch at the corner of his mouth. 'I must confess that's true, very true. But how is it so terrible?'

'You must very well know. A woman, especially one with no fortune, is expected to marry well, or to live forever in reduced circumstances, as a female companion or a governess or some such thing.'

There was a small silence which Phoebe had no intention of breaking.

'Is your position here so untenable?'

Too late, Phoebe realised how like an ungrateful wretch she must have sounded. 'Well, no, you know that it is not. But if I had been born a boy, I could have joined the military, gone into the church — although I'm not sure I would have suited. But as a mere female none of those things are possible.'

Phoebe heaved a sigh. 'You have not the least notion of how mad it makes me that I never had the chance of education like my brother, Charles. He was at Harrow, you know and then at Oxford just like Papa before him.'

Mr Prendergast raised a cynical eyebrow. 'If you have a leaning t'wards the church — surely there's still the nunnery?'

Aghast, Phoebe looked at him, then caught the glint of amusement in his eye and let out a chuckle.

'All things considered,' said Theo, his brooding features struggling to remain serious, 'I think you'd do better to concentrate on the marriage option.'

Immediately Phoebe's expression darkened. 'That's what Charles thinks. Trouble is I am not one who could sit and spend her time in embroidering slippers for any man.'

Mr Prendergast gave a visible shudder. 'Let me enlighten you. I can assure you that not all men have embroidered slippers.'

They said no more then, as they were fast approaching the stables and after watching Phoebe alight from her horse, Theo reiterated that he would have the chestnut brought round within a couple of days.

Wondering briefly why Daniel Benton had been at Stone Manor when there was no music lesson that day, Phoebe decided she would be patience itself and never once look out of the window wishing she could be riding instead of attempting to paint.

By this time Phoebe had met Richard Steel the drawing tutor, several times and found him to be open and likeable and altogether amusing company. She held as few illusions as to her talent with a pencil as she did concerning her singing voice. But she was delighted to find that Kitty was highly capable of producing very pleasing, ladylike water colour sketches. Richard did not take his profession too seriously, but he had good cause to be gratified by the progress Kitty had made through his lessons.

The afternoon passed pleasantly enough, with Phoebe dreaming about the chestnut mare she was to exercise, and wondering whether Theo had put off his meeting with the estate manager until after lunch in order to take her riding.

She could hardly believe it to be true that someone of his disagreeable disposition should put himself out to such an extent, then found herself remembering the way he held himself on his mount, and the strength of his hands as he'd tossed her into the saddle.

Phoebe put a hand to her burning cheek. It must be the sun that was shining brightly through the school-room window that was making her feel so hot. Mentally she shook herself, and tried to concentrate on the matter in hand.

'Oh, this is hopeless.' She threw down her brush and looked at the disappointing mess on her paper. 'It's a waste of good paper and colour.'

Richard came up behind her. 'Don't say that. You're a trifle heavy handed maybe, but be patient and I'm sure you'll improve.'

'Well, it occupies the time at all

events,' said Phoebe. 'And Kitty's painting is really very good indeed.'

Kitty flushed with pleasure. 'Do you think so? I must say I do enjoy it no end.'

Phoebe raised her eyebrows. 'More than the singing with Mr Daniel Benton?'

The flush on Kitty's pale complexion became even more vivid. 'Well, not exactly . . . Mr Benton is exceedingly kind, but I worry because my voice is not the best.'

Phoebe laughed. 'I'm persuaded it cannot possibly be worse than mine. I sing sharps where the flats should be and vice versa. But I must concur, Mr Benton is very agreeable and handsome too.'

'I have to go now,' said Kitty in a strangled voice, before scuttling red faced, out of the door.

'That was unnecessarily cruel,' offered Mr Benton, who was standing close to Phoebe while they packed up their painting materials.

'Hardly cruel. Teasing perhaps. But I think Kitty could do with more teasing in her life. She has been altogether too sheltered.'

Richard's hand touched her fingers and did not move away. 'You, I collect, have led a life with fewer restrictions?'

Surprised, Phoebe's eyes flew to his face. Full of ardour, his eyes looked down into hers. 'Phoebe,' he said. 'I know our acquaintance is not of long standing . . . ' He leaned forward as though to kiss her.

There was a dry cough from the doorway. 'I must apologise for interrupting what I perceive to be a touching tableau, but I must remind you of your duties Miss Latimer, and you Mr Steel, of your place.'

Theo's voice was as cold as the glance, which swept them both. 'Phoebe, Kitty needs help in finding her vinaigrette, which she thinks may have been left in the arbour, perhaps you'll be good enough to assist in its recovery.'

To her utmost chagrin, Phoebe found

herself blushing like a school miss. 'No indeed,' she stammered. 'You — you, are mistaken in what you have thought.'

'Really, and what have I thought exactly? . . . Please go to Kitty directly. Oh, and do try not to be such a dead bore, Mr Steel.'

With a final indifferent glance in Phoebe's direction Mr Prendergast turned on his heel and left.

4

Helplessly, Phoebe stood inside the door to Kitty's bedchamber and listened to her laboured breathing. Surely when they'd shared the painting lesson, just a few hours ago, Kitty had been in good health? Annie, her poor old face creased with anxiety hovered by the bed, soothing Kitty's brow as she sat propped against high pillows fighting for breath.

As soon as she'd heard that Kitty had become so anxious about her missing vinaigrette, Phoebe had run from the house to the rose arbour and found it resting on the arm of the seat where earlier in the day they had sat together chatting. At that stage, when she'd had it returned to her, Kitty, although rather flushed, had had no problem with her breathing so Mr Prendergast had left for his own home in order to have tea with his boys.

'I'm trusting you to keep a watchful eye on Kitty,' he said in the same cold tone he'd used to her in front of Richard Steel. 'Although I'm persuaded this is nothing serious, I've learned in the past that episodes like this can suddenly escalate where Kitty is concerned. Don't hesitate to send for me if you are at all worried.'

Phoebe met his intense scrutiny head on. 'You need not doubt me. I will attend to 'my duties' as you put it earlier.'

For a moment Theo looked as though he would like to say more, but instead he picked up his riding gloves and half turned away.

'Mr Prendergast, wait just a moment. The situation you saw earlier — you misconstrued the circumstances. Mr Steel meant nothing; it was all in fun. Pray don't blame him. It was only a mild attempt at flirtation on his part — hardly a kiss of passion.'

'Rest assured, Miss Latimer, it's of no significance to me whom you kiss, how often or with how much passion. It is entirely your own affair.' Theo's casual glance hardly rested on hers, but Phoebe still managed to note a certain tense frown between his strongly marked brows, before he added, 'I was just somewhat startled by your lack of finer feeling in that you failed to repulse his advances.'

Phoebe felt a small moment of triumph in that she'd managed to annoy the very starched up Mr Prendergast. However, it would hardly do to let him continue in the assumption that Richard Steel's attentions would be welcome to her.

'Well, I was on the verge of declining his not very serious advances when you came in,' a naughty dimple appeared at the side of her lips, 'but then of course I'm mindful that I have my position to consider.'

Theo lifted a curious eyebrow. 'Your position?'

'Well, you advised me I have to be on the constant look out for a husband, did you not?'

Theo's lip curled. 'You are surely not considering the art master?'

Phoebe widened her eyes and met his horrified stare head on. 'Why not?' But she couldn't suppress the amusement from spreading to her face for long.

A strangled laugh forced itself from Theo's lips. 'You are a minx,' he said. 'I thought as much the first time I saw you . . . Have a care though, Kitty does not possess your sophistication, she has never learned to flirt. Do not encourage her to copy your behaviour.'

Phoebe's chin instantly lifted and her steady grey eyes sparked with indignation. 'Fudge,' she said scornfully. 'You're talking gammon and you'd know it if you gave yourself a chance to reflect. You've surrounded Kitty with a bunch of old fogies for I don't know, how many years. Then you introduce to her not one, but two, very attractive young gentlemen, in the guise of educators.

'Is your youth so far behind you that you have forgotten how young people feel and behave? You would be far better protecting Kitty against the resounding tendre she has developed for her music teacher, rather than preaching correctness of decorum to me. Let me inform you sir, I can handle greenhorns of Richard Steel's ilk with one hand tied behind my back and desire no help from you.'

Theo's eyes narrowed. 'So you perceive Kitty to have developed romantic notions towards Daniel Benton?'

'Nothing serious. But enough to put her in a dither and bring on an attack of the vapours when teased about it . . . '

More boot tapping from Mr Prendergast. 'And in your considered opinion this is one of those times?'

Phoebe nodded.

'We'll see then, what the morrow brings. I hope you might be right, but you have not seen Kitty when she's really unwell, as I have done . . . If he is indeed having a detrimental affect upon Kitty perhaps we should terminate Mr Benton's contract.'

'Oh no. Pray do not. That would be

the very last thing to do. It would set Kitty's heart against you and put her in the mopes and to no account.'

The granite-like expression faded a little from Theo's face and he allowed himself a small smile. 'So what would you suggest Miss Latimer?'

Quelling the uncertain feeling that Mr Prendergast was laughing at her, Phoebe squared her shoulders. He'd asked the question and she would give him her opinion. 'She needs more young company. She's mentioned friends of her childhood — the Carringtons — they live not too far from here I believe.

'From the way she speaks she was very fond of them. Why does she never see them now? She needs not always to be with people older than herself, constantly reminding her of how frail she is.'

For a long moment, they contemplated one another. Phoebe wondered why it was she had never noticed before that Theo's eyes had such depths to them. He was the one to look away first. He cleared his throat. 'Well, she's calm now, but I'll call tomorrow to check on her progress.'

Phoebe watched as he strode from the room, heard him call to the groom and moments later, clatter over the cobblestones set at the front of the house.

And now here she was wondering whether she had been wrong to think that Kitty's attack was no more than sudden panic at the thought that her passion for her singing instructor was a secret no longer.

But at last Kitty's breathing seemed a little easier, and Phoebe touched Annie on the shoulder and told her to take a rest as she would watch over Kitty for the next hour or so. Annie did as she was bid and Phoebe sat quietly by the bed listening to each one of Kitty's inhalations, until they became the regular breaths of slumber.

Gently Phoebe released Kitty's fingers from their grip on the vinaigrette and, wincing a little from the smell she replaced the silver stopper.

Despite Phoebe's anxiety, Kitty's relapse appeared to be of a temporary nature, and Phoebe very soon discovered that so long as the silver vinaigrette was within easy reach, Kitty rarely panicked and seldom had recourse to actually use it.

Before long the days at Stone Manor settled into a routine which, although not proving an existence the most stimulating kind, Phoebe found she was, in the most part, enjoying. She no longer questioned the fact that Theo Prendergast visited three, or occasionally four, times a week now, and often enquired as to whether Phoebe would like to ride out with him.

Firefly, the chestnut mare that Phoebe had agreed to exercise, turned out to be a high spirited but beautiful animal she had immediately fallen in love with.

It was on one of those expeditions, when Theo was riding a little ahead of her and warning her to look out for overhanging branches, just as though she'd never seen an overhanging branch before in her life; that Phoebe broke her resolve to be patient and content.

She glanced at Theo's stiff back. 'Why do you insist on being such a stick in the mud?' she asked drawing level with him. 'Harry and Tom are nothing like so pompous, I dare say they must get their spirit of adventure from their mother.'

A faint flush crept into Mr Prendergast's cheek. 'If you call behaving with discretion and decorum, being a stick in the mud, well perhaps you are right. I consider myself only to practise the common civilities.'

'Fudge,' said Phoebe. 'You're very nearly as bad as my brother and he's a stuffed shirt on a horse, if ever there was one, even Father was used to say. And if you're going to rate me for want of delicacy or some such thing, please don't trouble yourself, I know how sadly lacking I am in all things ladylike.'

Phoebe cast her eyes to the heavens and a delicious shiver ran through her.

She glanced over her shoulder at Theo. 'The first time I saw you I thought you would be a great goer even though your behaviour to me was monstrously uncivil . . . And now you are walking your horse as though you are on an expedition with your elderly maiden aunt.'

She saw Theo's face darken, and gave a saucy grin of amusement. 'Well, no-one will mistake me for your maiden aunt of that you may be very sure.' She kicked Firefly's sides and felt the power of the animal unleash itself as she took off across the rough grass of the field and up towards the blue horizon.

In spite of her impression that she was throwing all caution to the winds and racing off at a tangent, Phoebe knew very well where she was going as she had taken the same route on previous occasions when unfettered by Mr Prendergast's company. If this time she did urge her horse forward more speedily than usual and jump a ditch without stopping, it was only because she was aware of Theo thundering at her heels on his big black stallion.

Resisting an impulse to laugh at him over her shoulder, she urged her mount forward until she reached the brow of a rather tame hill, then she reigned Firefly in and was standing at her head, stroking her nose when Theo eventually brought Thunder to a halt alongside her.

For a while neither of them spoke, although Phoebe was aware of Theo's panting breaths and her own thudding heart. When finally she risked a glance at him she saw his expression was as black as she'd ever seen it.

Theo dismounted at speed and made as though to take Phoebe by the shoulders. Then he dropped his hands to his sides. 'You little fool — you could have taken a nasty fall . . . Even killed yourself. Firefly is quite capable of throwing you.'

Phoebe noticed that for all the icy calm of his words he was visibly shaking, perhaps she really had frightened him. She felt it prudent to create a little more distance between them and led Firefly into a turn. 'I assure you not . . . ' she flung carelessly over her shoulder. 'Well, maybe — if I'd been a young greenhorn.'

'Very well,' admitted Theo after an even longer pause. 'I will allow that you are no greenhorn.'

When she turned to face him she recognised a glint of respect in his dark eyes. 'Miss Latimer, you have been hoaxing me all this time. Why did you not tell me you were so proficient a horsewoman?'

'Would you have believed me?'

Theo turned his horse and Phoebe remounted unaided. Silently they made their way back at a gentle trot.

It was not until they were within sight of the stables at Stone Manor that Theo broke the quiet that was between them. 'It had occurred to me,' he said. 'That you have been with us nigh on a month now, yet you have not visited my home . . . I am giving a small dinner party at Fairfield at the end of the week.

Nothing extravagant. Some near neighbours, the vicar, the doctor who attended my father before his death and also attends Kitty. Oh and Kitty, of course. It is time she was treated in a more adult manner.'

Carefully, Phoebe digested this information. 'The Carringtons?'

Mr Prendergast pursed his lips. 'I'm afraid they are away at present.'

'Ah,' said Phoebe. 'And the average age of your guests?'

Theo flushed. 'You are correct, on occasion you are somewhat lacking in sensibility.'

'Yes,' agreed Phoebe demurely. 'And I'm sorry for it. I expect Kitty will be overjoyed at the prospect of dinner with her companion and guardian, and friends of his generation.'

'I am not so very old.'

'Not in years maybe. I am very sure you are not too much above fifty.'

Mr Prendergast cast her such a thunderous glance that for a moment Phoebe feared she had gone too far.

Then surprisingly he tipped back his head and laughed.

A smile spread across Phoebe's face. 'I was beginning to think you were unable to do that,' she said. 'Through some fault at birth perhaps.'

'For your information I am but one and thirty years . . . And have a care. Do not push me too far Miss Latimer,' replied Theo before galloping off in the direction of his home.

If Phoebe had thought Kitty would be less than excited at the thought of a dull dinner party at Fairfield, she was to be proved wrong.

'Mr Prendergast must indeed believe me to be grown up at last,' she exclaimed with shining eyes.

'Indeed,' agreed Phoebe dryly.

'Did he tell you the names of his guests?' queried Kitty. 'Not that it is of any consequence for I am very sure I will be acquainted with them all . . . I wonder,' she went on her eyes suddenly widening. 'I wonder if Mrs Leadbetter will attend.'

Phoebe replied that the name did not sound familiar and asked why she should be of particular interest.

Kitty cast an eye around to check that no-one was in earshot. 'Well, I heard Annie speaking to Mrs Manningtree only a few days ago and she indicated that it was high time Mr Prendergast were to find a new wife and the widow Charlotte Leadbetter would surely suit the part.'

'Really?' answered Phoebe in a tone that was carefully noncommittal. 'And what did Mrs Manningtree have to say to that?'

'Well, actually she said that in her opinion, Mr Prendergast was looking in an entirely different direction, then they saw me and Annie said 'little pitchers have big ears', just as though I were still in the school room!'

'Monstrously unfair,' said Phoebe laughing.

All the same, she thought to herself later that she would be quite interested to meet Charlotte Leadbetter.

5

After consulting with Kitty as to appropriate attire for a small country dinner party, Phoebe stood by her own wardrobe quite undecided as to what to wear herself. Should it be her serviceable, but to her mind exceedingly dull, grey dinner gown with the tight sleeves and modest net shawl collar; or her more risqué amber gown with its modish satin trim, which rather drew attention to her décolletage? The thought of Charlotte Leadbetter put her in mind to favour the latter.

So it was that a few evenings later, Phoebe surveyed herself in her glass and considered herself to look as well as she had ever done. 'You look lovely, miss,' said Susan, the maid, who had helped her with her gown and her hair.

'Hmm,' Phoebe was still considering changing to the grey, which was perhaps more fitting to a lady's companion. But after all she was a lady by birth if not by her present fortune, so why should she try to disguise that by dressing in modest, boring grey which had originally been purchased as a gown of mourning for her father?

She allowed Susan to thread a satin ribbon through her upswept curls and considered herself to be ready.

Kitty looked pretty in a rather insipid peach affair, which Phoebe immediately jollied up by declaring she had the very shawl and spray of artificial rosebuds in a darker shade, which would set the dress off to perfection.

The carriage ride to Fairfield was quite short and Kitty kept up an inconsequential chatter of conversation all the way. On arrival at the house itself, Phoebe looked round with barely disguised curiosity.

Although her expectations had been tempered by the magnificence of Stone Manor, which was by far the largest and most prestigious dwelling in the area, she was unprepared for the warmth and mellowness that exuded from the more modest building that was Fairfield.

It was still daylight as the carriage swept up the drive, and the house was bathed in early evening sunlight, but Phoebe could imagine the light of a hundred candles pouring from the mullioned windows of the great hall on a grand occasion, and spilling on to the outside gravel.

As a footman helped them from the carriage Tom came running up to them. 'Hello Kitty, hello Phoebe,' he panted, not the least impressed by the grandeur of the moment. 'Papa is inside of course, but I wanted to tell you Floss has had four puppies and I am persuaded you will want to see them right away.'

'Well,' began Phoebe. 'Although it's clearly of the first importance that Floss and the puppies are well, perhaps the thing to do is let her rest a little now.'

'Lord, Tom,' said Harry who had

arrived behind his brother. 'This ain't the sort of do when you can just take people off to the stables. You must know that.'

'Phoebe ain't 'people'. Phoebe is never more comfortable than in the stables — she told me so.'

There was a scattering of gravel as another carriage drew up behind Kitty's.

'Lord,' said Harry again. 'It's Mrs Leadbetter, we'd better make ourselves scarce.'

'Wait just a moment,' entreated Phoebe. 'Tom we'd love to see the puppies, perhaps I will ride over next week when they are bigger and stronger.'

Her reward was a radiant grin from Tom before the pair of them slipped off and round the side of the house.

Halfway up the steps to the open front doors, Phoebe turned to see a tall fair lady stepping down gracefully from a very smart equipage. She had a carrying voice which Phoebe had no difficulty in overhearing.

'Theo's brats,' remarked the lady over her shoulder to a companion. 'Tedious indeed, they have been allowed to run quite wild since their poor dear mother died, but they should both be sent to school before too long, I hope.'

The dinner party was a great success. Phoebe found herself positioned opposite Kitty and between the vicar and the doctor. The vicar, when he wasn't speaking about Greek architecture, showed a marked propensity to dwell on the illnesses of several of his parishioners, whilst the doctor clearly preferred to discuss music with Phoebe.

This Phoebe was only too willing to do as, although not being possessed of a tuneful voice, she played the pianoforte in a passable manner, had an appreciation of music besides attending many concerts in London.

Kitty's neighbour was a gentleman in his early thirties who had been introduced as Samuel Walton, and on the other side of him sat Charlotte

Leadbetter and then Theo at the head of the table.

On Theo's right and next to the doctor sat Emily Walton, Samuel's wife, who was a demure little lady without much conversation. Phoebe engaged all her skills in drawing Emily out and very soon discovered that despite her mousy appearance she was a horsewoman of some standing.

'Capital,' Phoebe remarked during a general lull in conversation. 'We must arrange for a ride out together some time. Firefly and I are anxious to explore the countryside further.'

The footmen were removing the first cover; Phoebe lifted her eyes from the table to find herself being scrutinised by Mrs Leadbetter. 'Firefly my dear? Forgive me, you did say Firefly — did you not?'

'I did,' replied Phoebe with a coolness she was far from feeling.

There was a stirring of interest from the other guests.

'Yes, Ph — Miss Latimer has kindly

agreed to exercise my chestnut for me,' interjected Theo smoothly.

Charlotte Leadbetter gave an arch smile. 'Indeed? Is there no end to your talents, Miss Latimer?' Mrs Leadbetter's glance, which swept every inch of Phoebe that was on view, hovered a fraction longer than necessary at Phoebe's neckline.

'It's very kind of you, and I am much obliged that you refer to my horse riding skills as a talent, for it is a pleasure to be allowed to ride so spirited an animal. But she is a wonderful horse and prodigious sweet tempered if handled correctly.'

There was an awkward hush around the table, and Phoebe gathered from Kitty's anguished expression that she had said something out of place.

'Then there was old Matthew Creek's second child, she had the very same inflammation of the lungs,' commented the vicar to no-one in particular.

'Really' questioned the doctor leaning forward as though this was the most interesting fact he'd heard in months.

Phoebe's puzzled eyes met the amused glance of Mr Prendergast. He gave a strangled cough and looked away.

At last the dinner party was over. Judging that as Kitty was so fresh from the schoolroom, Mr Prendergast would not expect them to stay overlong, Phoebe exercised all her diplomacy skills by prettily making their excuses as soon as the gentlemen rejoined the ladies.

She stood waiting in the great hall while Kitty went to find the shawl, which Phoebe had lent her earlier. Over the grand fireplace was the portrait of a lady with a somewhat serious gaze, sitting in a flower garden.

'Forgive me for staring — she was very beautiful.'

For a brief moment, Theo's eyes grazed the painting. 'No she wasn't,' he said shortly. 'Well, to me she was. But this portrait makes a doll of her. It is not how I like to remember her. Her eyes have been made too large, her mouth too small, in the fashion of the day I suppose. Her hair had a reddish tinge — like Tom's — and her smile was so similar to Harry's that I look at him sometimes and — well, I catch my breath.'

Theo stood looking out of the window with his back to her. Noticing the tense set of his shoulders, for once Phoebe was bereft of words. Then he turned to face her and she was surprised to find him smiling. 'Isabel would have loved tonight,' he said. 'She found people fascinating and a source of endless amusement. She would have found the conversation about Firefly exceedingly droll.'

'Well, quite why that should be, I cannot but . . . ' started Phoebe. Then, Theo's warning look left her words trailing to nothing.

Kitty and Charlotte Leadbetter entered the great hall together and, after a few commonplaces, farewells were made.

'It's been a pleasure to make your acquaintance,' remarked Charlotte extending a languid hand.

'Indeed,' agreed Phoebe politely.

'And prey what was all that about?' asked Phoebe of Kitty when they were sitting in their carriage once more and on their way back to Stone Manor.

Kitty gave a nervous laugh. 'Well t'was not your fault, for how could you know? Not long before you arrived here in Norfolk, Mrs Leadbetter insisted on trying Firefly, even though Mr Prendergast had expressly forbidden anyone to do so saying that only he could exercise her until she had learned some manners.'

'Did he refer to the horse or Mrs Leadbetter?' asked Phoebe innocently.

'The horse of course . . . Oh, you are funning! Well, Mrs Leadbetter bade the groom to saddle her up once, when Mr Prendergast was called away to attend one of Tom's scrapes, I believe.'

'And?'

'And she'd barely covered four paces when Firefly threw her. I believe she landed in very unpleasant circumstances where the stable lads had not yet cleared up.' Kitty put her hands to her face.

'Oh dear,' said Phoebe. 'No wonder Charlotte Leadbetter regarded me as one she would like to kill.'

She smiled a little to herself, for despite Charlotte Leadbetter the evening had been convivial and the spark that had stirred in Theo's eyes as he greeted her had made her heart skip a beat.

Then her smile faded as she remembered the reported conversation Kitty had overheard between Annie and Mrs Manningtree. Surely Mr Prendergast did not intend matrimony with someone of Charlotte Leadbetter's ilk.

6

Slowly the days turned into weeks, and suddenly Phoebe realised that nearly two months had slipped by with her hardly noticing, or indeed missing the bright lights and whirl of town life.

Now lessons had finished for the summer, Mr Prendergast often brought his sons with him on his visits to Stone Manor. On the days when he was too busy to ride with her, Phoebe would allow them to show her parts of the estate they thought she'd not yet discovered and to lose her, again, in the delights of the maze. Occasionally, she'd share Kitty's music and water-colour lessons but, while the weather was good, preferred to be outdoors with Harry and Tom.

'I'm going away at the end of the summer,' said Harry importantly, on their way back from a stickleback hunting expedition.

'Oh?'

'Going to Harrow — in September.'

'That's good. Isn't it?'

'Lord yes. Can't wait. I'll meet no end of good fellows . . . Only . . . '

'Yes?'

'You'll still be here, won't you?'

Harry's face with its sprinkling of freckles looked anxiously up into hers.

'Well, I have no other plans,' replied Phoebe choosing her words carefully.

'It's Tom you see.'

Tom was presently engaged in stalking a kitten through the outskirts of the copse and was out of earshot. 'It's on account of Tom I didn't go away to school earlier. Father said we needed each other for a while longer. On account of Mother — d'you see?'

Phoebe nodded.

'It's two years now, so Father thinks you see, that Tom's all right now.'

'Well, I expect he's right then.'

'Lord yes. That's what I think too. Well, mostly anyway.'

'Harry? You do want to go, don't you? To school I mean.'

'Lord yes. I just wonder about Tom a bit and . . . '

'And?' prompted Phoebe softly.

'Well, Father says I'm very like my mother and he looks sad sometimes when he looks at me . . . I think maybe if I'm not here then he won't keep being reminded . . . Well, you know.'

Phoebe felt her throat constrict. 'Something I do know, Harry. Tom is a very lucky boy to have a brother like you and your father is a very lucky man to have two good sons to make him proud. I think you should go to school and enjoy it. You'll do very well.'

Harry's face flushed. 'You won't forget Tom will you? Only Father is sometimes so busy.'

'I won't forget,' promised Phoebe.

'Got him.' Tom caught up with them and held out his hat, which held a squirming, mewing kitten. 'D'you think Kitty would like him?'

'Kitty can't go near cats, you know

that,' said Harry scornfully. Then seeing Tom's face drop. 'You'll have to take it to the stables and one of the stable lads will look after it.'

Tom looked up beseechingly. 'You don't think Papa . . . ?' he started.

'No,' said Harry firmly. 'We've already an army of cats and dogs. You know full well there's to be no more. I'm surprised he's going to allow you to keep Flossy's last puppies — they're such ugly looking things.'

Phoebe placed an arm on Tom's shoulder. 'Come on Tom, we'll do as Harry suggested and take him to the stables — it's probably where it came from in the first place.'

When Phoebe had divested herself of kitten hairs and the dust of the stables, she joined Kitty and Annie in the downstairs parlour for some refreshment. Kitty had completed a painting that afternoon and Richard Steel was enjoying a glass of beer with them before he left.

Phoebe took a seat next to Annie.

Since Richard's display of feelings for her, she'd taken good care not to be alone in his company, not for fear of any repeat performance, but because she didn't want to be the unknowing cause of him losing his position. She watched now as Kitty and Richard stood looking critically at the painting in the light of the window.

Surely, Kitty's animated face, sparkling eyes and pure joie de vivre, couldn't be masking a sick disposition?

'Kitty looks so well, don't you think?' she asked Annie quietly.

The old lady nodded. 'It's always the same though. Just when she looks her best — she takes ill again.'

Impatiently Phoebe clicked her tongue. 'Oh how can that be? I won't listen to you.'

Annie gave a tired sigh. 'It's always the same. I've worked here all my life and no-one in this house pays me the least regard.'

Curiously Phoebe gazed at her, an old lady fast approaching seventy, who had nursed Kitty and Kitty's father before her. 'Annie, what was Kitty's mama like?'

An expression of sadness flitted across the nurse's features. 'She had a lovely disposition. Very like Kitty's. But she just faded away too.'

'Kitty is not fading away,' said Phoebe, fear making her low voice sharp.

Annie pursed her lips and Phoebe relented a little. 'I'm sorry, but I want Kitty to be well, like she is now — all the time . . . Did her mother have the same breathing troubles as Kitty?'

'Oh yes. She came here as a wisp of a girl; always looked too fragile to bear children . . . Surprise us when she did. Master David, Kitty's father, was so happy when Kitty was born, even though he would have liked a boy. But Kitty's mother was never as strong as Kitty. In childhood, to be sure, Kitty did seem to be a little chesty albeit she was never as poorly as her mother, but she did take cold easily.

'Then over the last few years we allowed ourselves to think she was growing out of her childhood maladies.' Annie gave a sigh. 'She so wanted to go to London last year — it seemed excessively mean to disallow it. So, against my advice mind, Theo took her to his sister's for the season . . . ' Annie lowered her tone to a bare whisper. 'Next thing, she was desperately ill, fighting for her life . . . We could have lost her, you know.'

'And these breathing difficulties, have they always been in the family?' asked Phoebe after a suitable pause.

'On her mother's side you mean? I think so, although there was her grandfather's brother, Matthew, the one who fought the duel, I believe he had the same sort of problem but then, that was on her father's side, of course.'

Momentarily diverted from her initial inquiry, Phoebe's eyes glittered. 'A duel?' she exclaimed. 'Dear me, how excit . . . I mean — how very shocking! Pray do tell what happened?'

Annie's face took on a confiding expression. 'It's not for me to say, but I do believe,' her voice sunk to a loud but conspiratorial whisper. 'A man was killed! Ooh yes — bled to death . . . '

'How very terrible. Was there much blood?'

'Terrible — yes, poor Matthew had to flee the country — until the dust settled.'

'Yes?'

'Well, eventually the dust did settle and it was forgotten by all but the family. But he was never heard of again.'

'Oh.' Phoebe felt rather let down. Where was the drama? Where the romance? Where the ending?

'Didn't anyone bother to look for him?'

'At first he wrote. But then when the letters stopped coming . . . ' Annie shrugged. 'He wouldn't be the first to go to the bad.'

Phoebe looked back at Kitty and saw that both she and Richard were now hanging on Annie's every word. 'Have you never heard the story before Kitty?' she asked.

'Yes, but I was never encouraged to speak of it.' Kitty came back from the light of the window and took a chair near Annie. 'I think, there was a lady involved. Father would never mention his Uncle Matthew.'

'Well, we've spoken of it for long enough,' pronounced Annie looking as though she was uncomfortably aware that she could be accused of gossiping.

It was just as well, because as Annie stopped speaking, Theo strode into the room.

'I've come to take my leave of you,' he said after admiring Kitty's painting and downing a small glass of beer.

'Harry and Tom left for home some half-hour ago,' volunteered Phoebe. 'And as you see you've already managed to frighten Mr Steel away,' she added as Richard left the room.

Mr Prendergast's stony expression didn't soften, but Phoebe had grown used now to searching for the twitch at the side of his lips, which sometimes gave away his amusement. 'I can't think why that might be,' he said. 'But at any event I won't be here for the next week, so will be unable to frighten anyone.'

'Oh?' Although conscious of a sudden heaviness of heart.

'I have to go to London on business. I'm taking Harry and Tom to stay with my sister. It will make a good change for them from rattling around here like a couple of country bumpkins.'

For a moment Phoebe wondered whether a 'couple of country bumpkins' was Charlotte Leadbetter's terminology and whether she would also be in London for the week.

Kitty very prettily wished him a happy journey and to please remember her to his dear sister. While Phoebe struggled hard not to feel absurdly jealous that on a whim, Mr Prendergast was able to decide to go to London, where she was trapped here in dreary Norfolk, with its wide skies and flat, wind scorched fields, and die of tedium.

'Phoebe, a word.'

Phoebe wondered for a moment whether to bob Theo a curtsy to make her feelings on being addressed like a servant plain, but after all what would be the point when it was clear that was precisely how he perceived her?

'Kitty looks well recently,' said Theo when they were alone in the hall.

'So I was saying to Annie.'

'I think in a large part it has to do with you,' went on Theo as though the words were being dragged from him against his better judgement.

'Am I to take it, I have done something of which you approve?'

Theo gave a thin smile. 'I am relying on you to continue to be vigilant. Kitty's welfare is very close to my heart.'

'I know that it is.'

'Also my best chestnut mare, Firefly. I hope I can rely on you to exercise her well and with regularity. You know Firefly will only allow the very best of horsewomen to sit upon her back.'

The smile widened and at a stroke his customarily serious face looked younger and Phoebe was allowed the glimpse of a more carefree Theo. What a pity the glance was so fleeting, that Theo was a devastatingly attractive man.

'You know that you can,' answered Phoebe, turning away before he might see her thoughts from her eyes.

'Also, I think we might act on your suggestion of arranging younger company for Kitty. She did well at Fairfield, I was very proud. Maybe on my return I'll solicit your help in planning a small gathering . . . An evening of conviviality — nothing wild of course.'

'What leads you to imagine anything I would arrange would be wild?'

'Goodbye, Phoebe,' said Mr Prendergast after a glance heaven wise and another of his disturbingly attractive smiles.

Phoebe was left in the empty hallway, wondering rather, why her heart was beating so fast and why she'd hoped for at least the touch of his hand before he was gone.

Just two days later when even a long ride on Firefly had failed to lift Phoebe's spirits; she came back from the stables to find Kitty, in a high state of excitement.

'Heigh-ho, what's afoot?' she queried in an imitation of Harry's manner.

'The Carrington's footman had delivered us an invitation to a — you'll never guess Phoebe . . . ' Kitty's words were tumbling over each other in her exuberance, ' — to a small country dance.'

'My word!' Phoebe tried to activate more enthusiasm into her voice than she felt.

'Only Annie says I should not go.'

Phoebe peeled off her riding gloves. 'Does she indeed, and why not pray?'

'She says I look feverish and that dancing would be too much for me and that Theo would not like it.'

'Well, of all things. I'll talk to Annie, don't you worry. Just give me a chance to change out of my riding dress.'

Half-an-hour later she was reading the invitation, which had come in the form of a letter from Mrs Carrington. The letter indicated that the family had only just returned home after being away for some weeks, or they would have called before in order to welcome Kitty's friend.

Mrs Carrington hoped very much that Kitty and Miss Latimer would be able to attend the small party they were holding in three days time. It was only to be a modest affair, but it was expected there would be enough couples to get up a country dance or two.

'Surely Annie can't be so disobliging as to disallow me to go,' wailed Kitty who did indeed look alarmingly flushed.

'Stop getting yourself into a pet over nothing,' ordered Phoebe. 'If you do indeed wish to go, you have to stay calm, eat properly, take fresh air, not give yourself the headache with your perpetual embroidery, and at all times assume that of course you are going. Why should you not? The Carringtons live only a small way away and are old friends. I am persuaded that even Th — Mr Prendergast would allow it.'

At her words Kitty did indeed become less agitated. 'I don't know that he would. I couldn't go to the last one.'

'Well, there must have been a reason . . . You must have been unwell. But now you are in the pink again. Anyway, it will be quite a dull affair I'll warrant. The exchange of a few commonplaces, a little light refreshment, and a couple of tame country dances — hardly a night of wild festivities . . . Now stop looking mulish, and let's look at your gowns. It will be a novelty to see you out of spring muslin and into a dress for dancing with satin, rosebuds and ribbons.'

In the event, Kitty wore a puffed sleeved dress with a high waist. It was pale blue, with floating ribbons and row upon row of frills round the ankles. Phoebe had brought two or three modest evening dresses with her, which were out of vogue in London now, but which she knew would still be considered quite modish in the country.

She eventually settled for the most frivolous — a rose pink round gown, which sported rather less in the way of ribbons and frills than Kitty's pale blue, but the simple cut of which she fancied made her appear taller. Her dark curls she wore in an upswept style which suited her small face.

Kitty was almost speechless with excitement, but when she first set eyes on Phoebe she gave a gasp of admiration. 'You — you look like a princess,' she stammered.

Phoebe laughed. 'A poor princess indeed,' she answered. 'But you Kitty are like a lovely fairy escaped from fairyland. Now, are we ready?'

Annie stood in the hallway with a cape and an extra woolly shawl over her arm. Every fold and tuck of her person exuded disapproval. For a moment Phoebe suffered a pang of contrition.

'Annie how very good of you,' she said taking both the cape and the shawl. 'I have already arranged for an extra blanket in the carriage should the weather become chilly, but we'll take these as well. Now, we shall not be late so never fear. And I think you'll agree Kitty will be the belle of the ball.'

A sniff escaped Annie's tightly compressed features.

'Please Annie,' entreated Kitty softly. 'You know how much I have missed my friends. It will be delightful to see them again and I am sure you wish me well really. Don't let me go with your face still so cross, for Phoebe will take care of me, and oh, I want to go above all things, but not if it upsets you so.'

At a stroke Annie's face softened. 'Enough of your flummery,' she said giving Kitty a quick kiss on the cheek. 'Now be gone with you. You have your vinaigrette in case the dancing brings on your breathlessness. But I'm sure all will be well, and the next thing will be, you'll be telling me all about it.'

Phoebe gave a sigh of relief as, careless of squashing her rosebuds; Kitty gave the old lady a hug before proceeding Phoebe out of the door to where the carriage awaited them.

The entrance of the Georgian mansion, typical in its Palladian symmetry, was suffused in the light of many flaming torches. A wave of anticipation swept through Phoebe as liveried footmen helped them from their carriage and up the front stairs to be welcomed by their hostess. Mrs Carrington, was an amiable looking woman who could not have been much above forty.

Some ten years older, her husband who was by her side, wore the countenance of one whom would rather be in his study with his books, and a glass of brandy. But Mrs Carrington greeted them warmly, kissing Kitty on the cheek and telling her she was in great good looks, then calling over to Hugo her eldest son, to only look how grown up Kitty had become.

'C-capital to see you Kitty. M-must

say you look in famous shape,' a clearly overcome Hugo stammered.

Kitty blushed delightfully and Phoebe heaved a sigh of relief because she could sense that the evening was destined to go well. Indeed she was more than pleased that bossy Theo Prendergast wasn't there after all, to spoil it for them.

The party went much as Phoebe had predicted. She found herself able very easily to slip in with the company, most of whom were of her own age or younger. There were also a few dowager chaperones and of course the local vicar, whom Phoebe had met at Fairfield. Mrs Carrington quickly pointed out that not only was he quite presentable to look at, certainly not much above forty, but — how very fortuitous — also a bachelor.

For a moment Phoebe wished Theo was present so she could wonder, for his ears alone, whether he were afflicted with the gout, as in her experience most bachelors of her acquaintance on reaching that age almost always were.

Instead, she smiled sweetly and

resolutely put Theo Prendergast out of her mind and her heart.

'Did you indeed enjoy it?' Kitty's face was pink with animation and her eyes sparkled with happiness on the way home.

'I did Kitty, I did. I enjoyed it so much in fact that I quite forgot the time, I only hope that Annie is not sitting up like the wicked stepmother, ready to welcome Cinderella home.'

'Oh no, d'you think she will be? No, I can see you are only funning.' Kitty sat back against the cushions of the carriage and gave a happy sigh. 'Did you not think it was the most convivial evening?'

'Most convivial.'

'And was not Hugo Carrington so very good looking? His blue cloth coat and white waistcoat so fashionable?'

'Certainly. And wasn't he most attentive?'

'Well, we are old friends I'm sure there's nothing very peculiar to be seen in that.'

'No indeed. I'm persuaded it would have been strange indeed had it not been so, you being by far the prettiest girl there.'

'You're hoaxing me again.'

'No, Kitty you looked very well, and you enjoyed the dancing, did you not?'

Kitty's eyes misted over. 'Oh yes, it's been so long since I danced, I had forgotten how enjoyable it can be.'

Phoebe smiled. 'So had I.'

Shyly Kitty glanced at her. 'Did you find dancing with the vicar blissful?'

'Blissful, is perhaps too strong a description,' answered Phoebe her eyes glinting with amusement, 'but he is a worthy man, and has a great deal of conversation — especially where Greek architecture is concerned.'

'Oh dear, poor Phoebe, were you bored?'

'How could I be bored? It was a preferable subject to the health of his parishioners. I loved watching you enjoy yourself, and Mrs Carrington is such an amiable creature. As you said, the evening was most convivial. I found it delightful. And moreover it will be only polite for us to return the hospitality extended to us and arrange a small party of our own.'

Phoebe had thought it to be impossible for Kitty to become any more animated. But on hearing her words, Kitty clasped her hands together with such an expression of happiness on her face that Phoebe felt a pang at how very dull her life at Stone Manor must be for her young companion.

'Oh, can we? Can we really? That would be famous above all things. Hugo says he will be here much more often now he is down from Oxford.'

'Good, then he will be able to come.'

'Oh yes, I would like that above all things,' said Kitty softly. 'You know — Daniel Benton is very romantic and melancholy with his long white fingers and his dark hair and thin face, but I declare that Hugo is more . . . '

'Fun?' prompted Phoebe.

Kitty smiled before sinking into a

private reverie which lasted until the carriage swayed into the drive and eventually to a stop outside her home.

'Hello, what's this?' It only took a moment for Phoebe to recognise Mr Prendergast's horse being walked on the cobbles at the foot of the wide entrance steps.

Sure enough once they were inside they were informed that Mr Prendergast was waiting in the drawing room. Phoebe felt no misgivings; in fact she was expecting to be congratulated on her initiative in chaperoning Kitty to the party in his absence.

Conscious of an unexplained fluttering in her heart, Phoebe swept into the drawing room. 'Good evening, Mr Prendergast, we did not expect you back so soon.'

Theo looked up from where he was leaning against the buttress end of the mantelpiece. 'No, that much is indeed obvious,' he said in a voice bordering on the frosty.

The warmth died out of Phoebe's

smile and Kitty looked agitated and felt anxiously in her reticule for her vinaigrette which, Phoebe noted, she had not used once during the evening.

'I don't know what we might have done to displease you sir, but I can assure you we have had a successful evening and you shall not spoil Kitty's enjoyment of it.'

'Then Kitty had best go to bed. She looks sorely tired, poor child. I hope the exertion has not been too much.'

'No, I have had a won . . . ' started Kitty.

'I'm sure,' interrupted Mr Prendergast. 'But the time is late and you need your sleep.'

After an agonised glance in Phoebe's direction, Kitty crept from the room.

He turned towards Phoebe. 'Now, perhaps you will explain yourself.'

Phoebe squared her shoulders. 'I have nothing to explain. Kitty received an invitation. No, we received an invitation. I knew you would not disapprove of our going to the Carringtons. You as good as said so before you went to London. How was your visit, by the way?' she went on with exaggerated politeness. 'I do hope it was agreeable, it is so very refreshing to have a break from routine — is it not?'

'You took Kitty to an evening party with no chaperone,' said Mr Prendergast in icy tones.

Phoebe's eyebrows shot up under her modishly arranged curls. 'I am not considered experienced enough to act as chaperone? That surely, is the whole point of my being here?'

An exasperated sigh escaped from Theo's lips. 'Phoebe, you are barely out of the schoolroom yourself. How can you be considered a chaperone? It was lucky it was only a small gathering or it would be all over the county that the two of you were junketing around the countryside unescorted. That is not a good impression to foster. Certainly not for my ward, nor would I think for someone like you, who still had expectations of making a tolerable match . . . You know my top priority is Kitty's welfare, but I have her reputation to think in addition to her health.'

It was hard to swallow back her immediate reaction, which was to leave the room without another word, and abandon Stone Manor next morning, but somehow Phoebe managed it.

Her slim fingers played with the clasps on her reticule and only when she felt she had control of her wayward temper did she look up and find herself staring straight into Theo's unsmiling eyes.

She took a deep breath. 'It does you credit sir that you are so protective of Kitty. However, let me reassure you — our evening caused no raised eyebrows, in fact Mrs Carrington complimented me on the fashion in which I made myself responsible for Kitty. Maybe you have let too long go by without mixing in modish society if you think a female companion of my background and age an unsuitable chaperone . . . '

It was Mr Prendergast's turn to drop his eyes. 'I was not implying . . . I mean — it is not that I don't consider you an able person . . . ' He broke off angrily. 'It is just that I did not expect you to receive such an invitation, or indeed accept it . . . You both look so young; scarce any difference in age to signify . . . I don't express myself well. Perhaps I overstate the case, but with Kitty's health being so unpredictable . . . '

His words tailed off into a smouldering silence.

'It was a very select gathering,' said Phoebe hastily. 'Only sons and daughters of genteel folk and, of course the vicar.'

'Ah yes. Let's not forget the vicar.'

Phoebe would not allow herself to be sidetracked. 'However, you speak of Kitty's health and I have to say Mr Prendergast, I am not quite happy about the nature of her illness.'

A quizzical lift of an eyebrow was the only response Theo gave.

'No indeed, hear me out. She seems

well, I mean really well. As robust as you or I, then for no apparent reason, she may have a small headache, a feeling of giddiness, a sore throat or a chill which neither you or I would consider of the first consequence. But Kitty, with her history of ill health, immediately takes to her bed with her beloved vinaigrette and becomes rapidly worse.'

'And your point?' asked Theo in a cold voice.

'My point? Is it not possible that she is indulging herself in a fit of the vapours and making herself ill by suggestion alone?'

Mr Prendergast raised a sardonic eyebrow. 'And do we have to now add physician to your list of attributes?'

A tide of colour flooded Phoebe's face. 'Perhaps 'concerned friend' would be a better term. Heaven knows, in this household Kitty could surely do with one . . . Now, I'll wish you goodnight sir.' Shaking with fury, Phoebe turned away.

'Wait.'

She was halfway to the door before his terse voice reached her. 'I called on your brother on my way from London. I have a letter from him for you and also one from your sister-in-law.'

Unwilling to let him see the angry tears standing in her eyes, Phoebe remained with her back to him.

The letters were pushed into her hand. A fire leapt in her heart at his touch.

'Thank you,' she managed in a voice so strangled, she was unable to ask why he'd thought to call on her brother without first mentioning his intention to her.

'I'll ride over tomorrow, I have business with the estate manager. Goodnight, Miss Latimer.'

Still burning, Phoebe made no reply.

7

Much to Phoebe's chagrin, the next morning seemed to prove Annie and Mr Prendergast correct in their assumption that an evening's frivolity would hold repercussions for Kitty.

Phoebe had spent a fitful night wondering in turn how Theo could be so aggravating and unreasonable, and then just why it should matter so much to her, when he was — well, so aggravating and unreasonable! Then she had her letters to think about too.

Her brother had never been the most fluent of letter writers and his missive had been short, starchy and to the point. He was glad she was settling in so well and that Mr Prendergast considered her to be a good influence on Kitty. Phoebe had to grin at this and wonder what her brother would make of the last interview she'd had with Theo.

Eliza's letter was very different in tone.

My dear sister, it started which had the effect of making Phoebe cringe.

I am so very delighted to understand that you are acquitting yourself above par at Stone Manor. Phoebe could almost hear the surprise in Eliza's voice as she read on. *It seems Kitty thinks highly of you and so too, does Mr Prendergast. Of course, Mr Prendergast is very much a gentleman and has such obliging manners, although I must admit I noticed that he is quite blunt in his speech and reticent about his private life. Not that I wish to impose upon a gentleman's most private thoughts, nothing could be less desirous of me.*

However, I am sure you cannot be unaware of your situation and how dependent you are on his approval. There was some talk of your position changing to something on a more permanent footing, but Mr Prendergast would not be pressed. So I do hope, dear Phoebe, you will be sensitive to this and not dismiss out of hand any proposition made to you, merely because you find country life to be a little mundane. You must think of your future, dear Phoebe, as I do constantly.

Phoebe yawned and set the letter aside. What on earth had made her think, even for a moment, that she could return to living as a charity case life, with Eliza in close proximity, reminding constantly of her 'position'? It would be insupportable.

No, she was better off here, caring for Kitty, playing with the boys, riding Firefly and yes, even tolerating the impossible Mr Prendergast with his strange ideas of putting her position on a more permanent footing.

All these thoughts fled from her mind, however, when, upon rising, she learned that Kitty was not feeling quite the thing and therefore partaking of breakfast in bed. Phoebe helped herself to a substantial breakfast then made her way to Kitty's bedchamber.

'How's this then, Kitty? You have to be in fine fettle in order to prove Annie, and Mr Prendergast, wrong.'

Kitty struggled upon her pillows. 'I know it is very poor spirited of me. I was well last night, and had my vinaigrette with me on my side table to reach for in the night, but then this tightness in my chest started and nothing seems to relieve it.'

'I'll have Anne bring you some hart's horn in water to sip. You must just sit here quietly until you feel better, which I'm sure you will by the time Mr Prendergast comes later this morning.' Phoebe picked up the silver vinaigrette. 'Try not to use this for a while, Kitty. Give the hart's horn a chance to work unaided and have a sleep. I'm persuaded you will feel better soon.'

After speaking to Annie, Phoebe made for the stables. She did not intend to be available when Mr Prendergast paid his visit.

Firefly was restless this morning so, on reaching an open stretch, Phoebe gave her her head for a while, only reining in when she recognised Theo's horse, Thunder, approaching.

He drew level. 'Good morning. I hoped I'd happen across you.'

'Well, as you see, your wish has been granted. Here I am.'

'Are you always so flippant, Phoebe?'

'Almost always. Are you always so serious — Theo?'

He laughed at the emphasis she put on his name and pulled his mount round so that they rode together.

'I expect you've come to rate me because Kitty is not feeling quite the thing today. No doubt it is my fault as usual.'

'On the contrary. When I left her, she was dressed, sitting quietly, but looking forward to her singing lesson. Perhaps you are right when you say she is too often with old people. Indeed I may have to agree that we could be fostering hypochondria.'

Unable to resist feeling just a little victorious that she had persuaded him to her way of thinking Phoebe gave a small smile. 'And what do you propose the remedy for that may be?' she asked.

'Perhaps we could think about drawing up a list of guests for a small party of our own?' he suggested tentatively. 'I think it would quite occupy Kitty's mind for the immediate future. Stop her from dwelling too much upon her own health . . . Although it's hardly surprising that she should, with Annie watching for the least sign of illness, which maybe, I must confess, something I, too, have been guilty of.'

A frown appeared between Phoebe's eyes. 'Indeed, but it's not that alone. It cannot be good for her when all around her people are dying young. Well, relatively young, and all talk is of illness or death. Both her parents were dead before reaching forty. Both my parents are dead, although of course, Papa married late in life, and my mother was carried off by pneumonia — in spite of being by nature as robust as I. Then, your wife Isabel, forgive me, but she died I believe in childbirth?'

Silence. Phoebe cast a sideways look at Theo's expression, which was tight and thunderous.

'You presume too far.'

His profile looked dark and forbidding.

Phoebe took a deep breath. 'Forgive me, but that's precisely the attitude that does Kitty so much harm . . . No, hear me out. Harm to your boys, too. Isabel is never mentioned. Why can you not talk to them as you did to me, of how precious her memory is to you? Those boys need to be reminded she existed and that you did indeed love her and that you remember her often with love, not sadness and certainly not bitterness.'

Theo turned in his saddle and furnished Phoebe with the most scathing of glances. 'Don't tell me, madam, that I don't hold my boys in the highest regard!'

'Well, I'm sure if you do, no-one would know it — least of all them. That they respect you above everything, is easy to see. But all they seemed aware of is your approval which, I don't have to tell you, is hard won; or your sensor, which is far more often apparent! D'you know what Harry thinks? He thinks you're sending him away to school because his likeness to his mother upsets you!'

Theo's lips firmed to a straight line and his eyes smouldered in his strained face. For a moment they stared at one another and Phoebe thought he would lean forward and strike her and that if he did — then maybe she deserved it.

'Enough!' He kicked his horse's sides and set off at a gallop.

Hopelessly, Phoebe watched. Still shaken from the pain and, yes, loneliness she'd glimpsed in his eyes, she admonished herself for once again being too forthright. If only she could take her words back — she should certainly have known better than to mention Isabel without invitation.

It wouldn't do for her to gallop after

him and apologise for speaking out of turn, which was what she would like to do. He would need time to collect himself, time to allow some of the sense of what she'd said to penetrate. But clearly Firefly, who had no finer feelings, was eager to pursue Thunder. She pawed the ground, itching to be away, and eventually Phoebe allowed her to edge from a walk to a trot.

On reaching the edge of the copse however, she found Thunder, riderless, champing at the tall grasses at the side of the bridle path. With some apprehension, Phoebe urged Firefly forward and on rounding an outcrop of trees, found a white-faced Theo stretched out full length on the ground in a lifeless-looking pose.

For a moment, Phoebe's heart left its usual resting place, jumped into her throat and threatened to choke her.

'Heavens above!' All female delicacy of feeling forgotten, she threw herself from Firefly's back and on to her knees beside Theo's prostrate form.

'Oh, no. Oh, please, God, no!'

There was no response from Theo. Her gloved hands were resting on his shoulders, her face very near to his. Her heart was pounding now — next to his. Perhaps it was his heart she could feel. She put her head to his chest, trying to feel for something to tell her he was alive. Her breath caught on a sob. 'Are you alive? Oh, please, please be alive.'

She was answered by a feeble flickering of Theo's dark lashes. 'I could hardly answer you if I were dead.' The beginnings of a smile tugged at the corner of his mouth as he struggled to sit up, then fell back again. 'Lord, I feel strange.'

'Just lie still till you feel more the thing . . . I, I apologise for all that I said. You were right to be angry . . . Only tell me, can you move your arms and legs?'

A strangled snort of laughter escaped Theo's lips. 'Phoebe, that's so typical of you,' he said faintly. 'First you tell me to lie still, then you ask if I can move.'

'Well, can you?'

Gingerly, Theo twitched his limbs a few inches in each direction. 'Yes, I'm sure that I can. Where's Thunder?'

'Never worry. He's feeding himself at the other side of the copse. When you're feeling sound again, I'll catch him.'

'I'm as right as can be — I do assure you. Please fetch him now. He went down a rabbit hole. He may be lame — front right fetlock.'

'You're more lame than he is,' said Phoebe when she led the horse back to where Theo was now half sitting with his head in his hands. She threw the rein over a tree branch. 'How do you feel now?'

'How do I feel?' He gave a wry grin. 'I feel ridiculous.'

'Yes, so I would expect, but apart from that. Do you think you can ride, or should I go for help?'

For this concern she received a glance that quelled at twenty paces. 'I perceive you would not like that?'

'Thank you — no.'

Phoebe's lips quirked into a sudden smile. 'I have to admit it's quite agreeable to have you at a disadvantage for once.'

'If my head were not swimming, I'm nearly sure I could give you a set down to end all set downs, but as it is, I cannot bother.'

Phoebe grinned again, sat down beside him and busied herself by making a daisy chain. Behind them the horses nuzzled at the grass, a magpie screeched and a soft breeze stirred the summer leaves. Rarely had Phoebe felt so peaceful. When the daisy chain was finished, she draped it round her neck, and seeing Theo was in no hurry to move, started on another.

Theo was very quiet, but presently she noticed that a little more colour was showing in his cheeks. She stared at the line of his cheek and at the sensual mouth, which was too often set in a straight forbidding line and found herself reluctant to look away.

Theo turned his head and for a moment his brown eyes locked on to her clear enquiring gaze. Almost as though unaware of what he was doing, he lifted a finger and placed it under her chin.

Phoebe stopped breathing. Then he looked away and gave a half laugh, removing his finger from her skin as though he didn't know quite how it came to be there. 'I sometimes think I must appear to you, and maybe others, as some kind of ogre.'

'Beg pardon?'

'I am very sure you heard what I said.'

Quickly, Phoebe pulled herself together and pretended to consider. '*Monster* is the word I would have chosen, but yes, ogre could apply.'

'I make no excuses. Other than to say it is difficult to lose someone you love . . . We married very young. Isabel was eighteen, I was twenty.' He gave a small smile. 'It was family approved. We were childhood sweethearts . . . '

He picked at a piece of grass and started to wind it round his fingers. 'Perhaps you are right about my boys, I should talk to them more. I kept Harry home, partly because they have grown so close, I thought it was for the best but also because I know how much I will miss him when he does go away to school.'

'Perhaps you should explain that to Harry,' suggested Phoebe softly.

'Yes,' agreed Theo. 'Perhaps I should. I've not thought of things from a young boy's perspective, I think. And perhaps I've been too strict in other ways. Always I am scared of being too soft, but I swear to you, I would never send Harry away, thinking to spare my own feelings. What a terrible thing that would be.'

Phoebe rose gracefully to her feet and extended a hand to help Theo as he gingerly tried his weight first on one foot, then the other.

'Men are all the same,' she observed. 'They never notice the things going on under their very noses.'

Theo looked down at her from what felt like a great height. 'I do.'

Phoebe gave an unladylike snort. 'You least of all ... Tell me then. Furnish me with one example.'

'You have a very fine pair of grey eyes, which sometimes take on a blue appearance, sometimes green — dependent maybe on your dress or your humour.'

For a long moment, Phoebe let herself stare into Theo's face as it hovered above hers, so near that she could see a nerve twitching at the side of his mouth. 'Do they?' she said faintly. 'Do they really?'

At that instant, Firefly chose to give vent to her impatience with a long snort of disapproval. It was enough to bring Phoebe to her senses. 'We had best make haste,' she said in a voice she wasn't sure was hers. 'For I think the fall has quite addled your brain.'

'It may well have done.' Theo kept an arm round her shoulder and leaned heavily against her until he reached Thunder's side.

'Do you need help to mount?' she enquired politely. 'Or will it be enough if I just hold him steady? Of course,' she added cheekily, 'I can put you on a leading rein if you should wish it.'

Sure enough, as Theo had said, Kitty appeared to be in the very best of health when they eventually arrived back, but although Theo appeared none the worse for his fall, he chose to lunch with the estate manager. Phoebe bit down a feeling of disappointment and listened again, but with only half an ear as Kitty rattled on about the previous evening's very agreeable entertainment.

After having partaken of the light luncheon, and Kitty had finally departed for her singing lesson, Phoebe was at last free to examine her own confused thoughts. She sat very quiet and straight for a few moments, struggling to remember the odious Mr Prendergast at his most odiously high handed. Finally, she sighed and gave up, recalling instead the touch of his hand on her chin; the serious yet warm expression in his eyes as he'd gazed at her.

She'd been too long in the country, that was the trouble; too long without entertainment, fashionable society and witty conversation. What was she thinking of dreaming about tame country rides with the serious-minded guardian of the sweet girl to whom she was companion?

And why would the wildly unreasonable and stern Mr Prendergast suddenly become — well, reasonable and yes, practically charming, all of a sudden? No, something was wrong. People didn't change their demeanour so quickly and for so little reason — did they?

She was becoming altogether too fond of the odious Mr Prendergast. Attempting to bring herself back down to earth, she looked round the comfortable surroundings to which she'd rapidly become accustomed, and her eye alighted on the silver vinaigrette sitting at the side of Kitty's sewing table.

On a whim, Phoebe unscrewed its top and took a deep sniff of the bottle's contents. It smelled of camphor and some other musky odour Phoebe struggled to name. Her eyes watered and she sneezed. Some sudden impulse made her stretch over, open up the sewing table lid and drop the vinaigrette amongst the tangled silks and cottons, where it sunk from sight.

'Oh, here you are.' Annie bustled into the room. 'Kitty was asking if you'd like to accompany her on the pianoforte later.'

'Of course,' answered Phoebe, still wondering what had prompted her action. 'No, don't go, Annie. There's something I wanted to ask you. Should anything happen to Kitty, or should she not marry or have children, do you know who would benefit?'

At her question, Phoebe felt as startled as Annie looked. The thought had hardly come into her mind than the words were out. Well, it was too late now. Curiously, Phoebe watched as the expression on Annie's face changed from surprise to one of supreme discomfort.

'Well, I'm sure I don't know why you would be asking such a question, Miss Phoebe, but I think it to be the case that the lawyers and Mr Prendergast would have to search for any relatives of the uncle I was telling you about. The one that went abroad after the duel and was never heard of again.'

Phoebe nodded. 'I see. And if they were unsuccessful? Who would stand to gain then?'

A shadow passed over Annie's features. 'In that case, there being no other living relatives, then I think Mr Prendergast would inherit.'

'Thank you, Annie,' said Phoebe in a cool voice that belied the sinking of her heart. 'There is no need to mention this conversation to anyone.'

'No, Miss,' replied Annie.

Later, whilst sitting at the pianoforte, Phoebe watched Kitty and Daniel's behaviour together. That they enjoyed one another's company was obvious, but it seemed Kitty had at last got over her crush on Mr Benton and now treated him with only a sisterly respect. Daniel, as always, behaved in a very proper manner, declaring that Kitty's voice was a deal stronger, but enquiring after her vinaigrette, for he knew how much she was attached to it.

'Oh, it's not far away,' interjected Phoebe hastily, inwardly cursing Daniel for his good manners, herself for her deceit, and Theo because she could no longer trust him. 'It was in the sewing room earlier. Please sing that again, Kitty, it was truly delightful.'

8

The next morning was humid and overcast. On the afternoon previously, once Kitty's music lesson had finished, Phoebe had been begged to spend the remainder of the day in the compilation of a list of friends Kitty would like to invite for their select evening party. Although the date of this had yet to be decided, Phoebe was only too happy to comply and so distract Kitty from any thought of retrieving the vinaigrette. It had proved exhausting employment.

At bedtime she fell asleep immediately and, despite her dreams being of a disturbing nature, involving Mr Prendergast and herself in all sorts of unseemly circumstances, slept without waking till morning.

Now, Phoebe tried to think logically about the dreadful notions that, this morning were slowly seeping back into her consciousness and was aware that she had some serious thinking to do both on her own and Kitty's account.

First, why was Theo so protective of Kitty, and so insistent that she was a semi-invalid? Why had he pretended that he would encourage Kitty to look up the friends of her childhood, then become so angry when he discovered Kitty had been to the Carringtons', when she's clearly enjoyed it and no harm had come to her?

Was it because he was really determined to make his young ward into a recluse? If that were the case, Phoebe argued with herself, then surely he wouldn't have arranged for her singing lessons and the drawing master's visits? Of course, he must be aware that Annie was always hovering around to keep an eye on things and perhaps he felt that it was safer for Kitty to meet with others only under her own roof and then, only those he had vetted first.

Phoebe caught her breath as she realised she was thinking in terms of safety. Did she really feel as though Kitty was under any threat other than that of her own poor health? Of course not, it was ridiculous. Why should anyone want to harm Kitty, and who would that person be?

Deep from inside herself, Phoebe rejected the question for melodramatic drama. Her rational mind told her she was being perfectly nonsensical. If Theo Prendergast was trying to protect his ward it was because, as Kitty had told her, he was an old family friend anxious for her welfare. After all, he'd also agreed for Phoebe herself, to join the household. Why would he do that if his intentions were anything but good?

But then, Phoebe asked herself, why exactly did he ride over to Stone Manor, sometimes as many as five times a week recently? Was he keeping a watch on her as well as Kitty? And why did every encounter between Mr Prendergast and herself seem to end up with one or both of them losing their tempers? Had he been trying to drive her away so he could prove to Kitty that he was the only person she could really rely on?

But why would that suit Theo? Where was his advantage, if Kitty were to spend the rest of her life as a pampered invalid?

All of which was why Phoebe had questioned Annie the previous afternoon and brought her back to the same answer. Suppose Theo had already tried to trace relatives through Matthew's line. Suppose he'd tried and failed. If Kitty were to die childless, and Theo was the next in line to benefit, then he would have plenty of reasons to encourage her in her belief that she was of sickly disposition, could not socialise, would never marry or have children.

There was a rumble of thunder, which Phoebe was oblivious to.

She was remembering the tender expression in Theo's eyes as he'd looked down at her. Was yesterday afternoon all a charade put on entirely in order to win her over; to earn her support? Surely that Theo, the gentle, sensitive Theo she had glimpsed for just a moment yesterday — that couldn't be a lie, could it?

'I won't believe it,' she said aloud, then despite the warm temperature, she shivered.

Later that morning, it was a quiet and subdued Phoebe who arrived at the old schoolroom. The threatened rain had still not materialised, but Richard Steel deemed it safer to paint inside, rather than risk a good soaking and ruined painting, out of doors. As Kitty bustled about collecting her painting equipment, she chatted with animation about Hugo Carrington.

'So Hugo I collect, is the new hero in Kitty's life?' Richard asked Phoebe quietly whilst Kitty was busy at the far end of the room setting up her easel.

'So it appears,' answered Phoebe woodenly. 'Although to be fair, she's known him all her life and, they've always been good friends.'

'No doubt Daniel will be relieved,'

said Richard. 'I think he was concerned that one day Kitty would fling herself at his feet and declare her love for him, which would mean of course, his position would be forfeit. Can't have your pupils falling in love with you. Not the done thing.'

'Oh I'm persuaded it wouldn't have come to that. Anyway, Mr Benton doesn't give the air of being poor, his clothes are good and he owns a horse, does he not?'

Richard Steel raised his eyebrows with surprise. 'Now, what makes you think that? No, he has lodgings at the village and hires a room to run his private lessons.'

The beginning of a frown was appearing between Phoebe's brows. 'But I have sometimes seen him at the stables?'

'That's as maybe. Perhaps he has a liking for horses, some fellows do. No, he walks here from the village, just as I do, unless I'm lucky enough to get me a ride on a farm cart part way, but it's a pleasant enough walk, I've never heard Daniel complain.'

After taking a moment to digest this information, Phoebe shrugged and started to lay her own equipment on the table. Covertly she studied him, wondering whether to take him into her confidence. He had an open friendly face and had never given her any reason to doubt his integrity.

'Mr Steel,' she ventured after watching him setting up Kitty's still life, which consisted of a bottle, a candlestick, a lump of cheese and a knife. 'How long have you known Kitty?'

Richard grinned at her over his shoulder. 'About five years I should say. I was a struggling artist then, but now I take private lessons, make quite a good living and still manage to paint and sell some of my own work.'

'Indeed? And how long have you known Daniel Benton?'

'Oh he's more recently on the scene. Arrived here some eighteen months ago. He teaches music two days a week at a local private school, but he was casting round for extra work, and I believe Mr Prendergast approached him.'

'I wonder why he should choose the village of Stone Manor?'

Richard returned his attention to the still life and adjusted the bottle to a less central position. 'I seem to remember his mentioning that his family originally came from these parts . . . Anyway, might I enquire — why the sudden interest in our life histories?'

Phoebe smiled. 'A vulgar curiosity. Sometimes I collect you seem to know much more about Kitty's family than they know about you.'

Richard laughed. 'Well, if you live in an area for ever, you can't help but know the business of the folk in the big houses — and my mother does like to rattle on.'

Kitty brushed past them, hurrying out of the door. 'I will be back presently,' she said. 'There is something I have mislaid.'

For a moment Phoebe paused, in two minds as to the wisdom of her next question. 'Please don't judge me, but I have a very particular reason for asking you — does Mr Prendergast ... I mean, I know he seems a man of substance, but oh — I have to ask it — how is his fortune positioned?'

The moment she'd stopped speaking, she regretted it. 'No, I should not have asked. Pray disregard it.'

But now she did have Mr Steel's full attention. His eyes searched her face, and she felt herself colour. 'So that's the wind of it? Well, he owns a fair part of Norfolk so he ain't short of blunt, you may be sure of that.'

Phoebe could have bitten out of tongue. Of course, Richard was bound to jump to the wrong conclusion. 'Mr Steel, you are wrong. I'm not hanging out after Mr Prendergast. Lord, nothing could be further from my mind. I have no thoughts in the direction of a match with anyone at the moment, besides we do not deal well together. I ask only because of how it may affect Kitty.'

Richard shrugged and turned away. 'As you say.'

Kitty burst back into the room. 'I can't find it. Annie and I have both searched.'

Phoebe felt her face colour again as she reassured Kitty the vinaigrette could not be far and that indeed she would go herself and see if she could find it.

What a sorry mess she had got herself into. Her face burned as she made her way to the sewing room and helped Annie in a search for an object, which she knew would not be found.

9

The storm broke at luncheon. Contrary to Phoebe's expectations, Kitty had accepted the vinaigrette's disappearance as a nuisance that would very soon be resolved, exclaiming that she could do without it at present and knew well, it must be either in the sewing room or her bedchamber, and would be sure to turn up soon.

Theo arrived shortly after lunch. Phoebe met him in the hall where he cast off his coat and beaver hat, which held a puddle of water in the brim. At the sound of her footfall he turned to greet her.

'Forgive me,' he said, his eyes seeming to light up at the sight of her, 'I am not expecting you to ride with me in this weather, I come to enquire after Kitty of course, and to discuss with you both arrangements for Kitty's party.'

Fighting the urge to give him a full answering smile and comment upon the fact that an *evening of conviviality* had now changed to a *party*, Phoebe could only nod politely. 'Kitty will be pleased I'm sure,' she said but with less than her usual enthusiasm. 'I will tell her you are here, she will be down directly.'

Theo gave her a piercing look from under his jutting brows. 'What's amiss?' he asked curtly.

Resolutely Phoebe returned his stare. 'Nothing. Nothing's amiss. Why must you always assume the worst? You will be glad to hear Kitty is well, her most pressing worry being the whereabouts of her silver vinaigrette, which I consider best lost, for all the good it ever does.'

Theo's eyes narrowed. 'I'm sure it will be found,' he said. 'But I was not referring to Kitty but yourself. You are looking out of sorts. Is everything well?'

'Yes, exceedingly so. All that is wonderful, I'm sure. I'll fetch Kitty.'

At that moment Kitty chose to walk

down the staircase, her head held high, her chin at a confident angle. Phoebe thought she'd seldom seen her in such good looks.

Theo too seemed momentarily overwhelmed at the sight of her. 'Well, Kitty a very good afternoon to you,' he said. 'Would you not agree Phoebe, Kitty looks quite the young lady.' He gave a mock bow and took Kitty's hand and kissed it solemnly.

A wave of misery washed through Phoebe, as she turned away. 'You must excuse me,' she said in a choked voice. 'Kitty will remember whom she wishes to invite. We compiled a list only yesterday. Now, there is something I must attend to.'

Aware that two puzzled pairs of eyes watched her progress, Phoebe reached the foot of the imposing staircase and cursing herself for a fool, through a blur of tears managed to make her way to the top.

She must have been blind not to see the obvious answer to all her questions.

Theo was playing for time. He was waiting for Kitty to grow up. It would be so very convenient. The two estates sat side by side. The boys were fond of Kitty and needed a mother.

Theo was going to kill two birds with one stone. Just as soon as he considered her to be old enough, he intended to marry Kitty himself.

The rain had been quite violent, but in the way of most summer storms, had passed over quickly, leaving blue skies and bird song in its wake.

Phoebe stared from the window of her room, knowing she could stay at Stone Manor no longer. She would go back to her brother, Charles and Eliza, and only then contemplate her future.

The thought of leaving almost wrenched her in two. Of course she would miss Kitty, miss Stone Manor, miss the boys and Firefly. Despondently, she dashed a tear from her cheek. And Theo?

But she couldn't think of Theo. Not without picturing him bent over Kitty's hand, pressing his lips to her fingers. Not without imagining them as a married couple.

They'll never suit, she thought. Kitty won't make him happy. He'll order her about and soon it will turn to bullying. She will be unhappy because she's not had time to have any fun, and Theo? Well, why should she care about Theo?

But she did. Pleading a small indisposition Phoebe took a light supper in her room and did not leave it again that day.

The next morning however, although she had hardly slept, she came downstairs and trying to appear as normal as possible, announced that she was feeling quite the thing again and intended to go riding immediately after breakfast.

'Please do be careful,' cautioned Kitty. 'Mr Prendergast was quite anxious — your being so unlike yourself yesterday.'

'Fiddlesticks,' said Phoebe picking up her leather riding gloves. 'He was very likely annoyed because I wasn't able to dance to his tune promptly.'

'No indeed. He was truly concerned and intends to come today to enquire after you.'

'Well then, you may tell him I am quite myself again and have gone riding by the canal,' replied Phoebe.

Quickly she walked to the stables, knowing that this would probably be her last ride on Firefly, and that she would have to take a different route from her much loved trek by the canal in order to avoid Theo, should he decide to check up on her.

The stable lads went quickly to saddle Firefly and Phoebe stood quietly beside George's stall, drinking in the atmosphere of one of her best loved places. Bees were buzzing in the honeysuckle, which snaked its way through the brickwork from outside, and the sounds of the horses, shifting and snuffling in their stalls had become very familiar, and very dear.

Wishing that her curiosity hadn't led

her to ask so many questions the answers to which she did not like, she blinked rapidly because for some reason her eyes were watering from the bright morning sunlight.

Suddenly, she heard footsteps. It couldn't possibly be Theo as he would be on horseback, but instinctively she stepped back into the shadows of George's stall, unwilling even if it were only a stable lad, for him to see her tears.

It was only Daniel Benton. Phoebe dashed the tears from her cheeks and swallowed, then she frowned, surely Kitty's lesson was not till the afternoon. Silently she watched as Daniel's eyes purposefully swept the yard. One of the stable cats was basking in the sunlight falling on a low brick wall. Smiling a little, Phoebe watched as Daniel went over and started stroking the animal.

George snorted and Phoebe absently stroked his nose. She was just about to call out to Daniel when she saw that he had collected a wad of cat's fur in his hand. Furtively he reached into his jacket for his wallet, stored the cat's fur away and with one more glance round the yard, softly left the stables.

What a strange fellow he was. Phoebe was quite relieved that Kitty had had a change of heart where he was concerned. She'd always preferred a forthright character herself, even if they sometimes appeared to be odiously overbearing — just like Theo Prendergast for instance.

'Whoa lady . . . She's a bit skittish this morning, miss.' One of the grooms trotted Firefly out of her stable and threw Phoebe up into the saddle. Patting Firefly's velvet neck, Phoebe thanked him with a smile and clattered out of the yard.

This was better. Once she was moving with the chestnut beneath her Phoebe, began to feel more optimistic. She couldn't be mooning round all day every day now, just because a certain Mr Prendergast was planning to marry a certain Miss Kitty Bellamy and chose to keep her on a short lead until he could decently do so. It had little or nothing to do with her. She slowed Firefly to a trot and cast her mind around for something other than the set of Theo's sensual mouth to contemplate.

So why was Daniel Benton visiting the stables at this time of day? Why was he visiting them at all? And what was this penchant he had with cat fur?

Totally unbidden a series of pictures flashed through her brain. Harry saying sternly to Tom. 'You know Kitty can't go near cats.' Kitty, eyes swollen, fighting for breath, the silver vinaigrette on her bedside table. The vinaigrette itself held up to the light, its murky depths unfathomable. And, could it only be two days ago? Daniel enquiring politely as to the whereabouts of Kitty's precious little bottle. It took only a few moments longer for the significance of what she'd seen to register.

Phoebe brought Firefly round in a wide circle and headed back towards the stables.

But why? Why would Daniel top up the vinaigrette with a substance he obviously knew Kitty was allergic to? Was he trying to keep her an everlasting invalid, so she wouldn't stray far from home and he would therefore keep his position? Was he in love with her? Did he really think there was any chance Kitty would marry him?

Or, was he trying to poison her?

The surprised stable lads looked up as Phoebe and a disappointed Firefly rattled back into the yard. 'I've changed my mind,' said Phoebe. 'Please ask one of the more able lads to exercise Firefly. There's something I have to do.'

10

By the time Phoebe reached the back
entrance to Stone Manor, she was out
of breath. She cut through the large
formal dining-room and barely stopping to register that Mr Prendergast's
hat and gloves were on a low table in
the hall she made her way to the empty
sewing room.

She knew there was a sharp quill
pen and some paper in the writing desk
in the corner of the room. Quickly
and quietly Phoebe opened the desk
and found them. Then she retrieved the
vinaigrette from where it nestled in
its hiding place amongst the tangle of
silken threads, and unscrewed the top.

'Phoebe, you are better, I wonder if I
might speak with . . . What on earth are
you doing?'

Mr Prendergast stood just inside the
doorway watching in astonishment as

Phoebe probed out the contents of the glass bottle.

A horrid mass was soon showing dark against the white of the paper.

'Good God, the stench is foul indeed.'

'Indeed,' agreed Phoebe looking up at him flushed with triumph. 'It is full of cats' fur mixed with ammonia and goodness knows what else. This recipe,' she pointed to the evil smelling mixture, 'this is why Kitty's health is so volatile. Although, I was never so informed — she is allergic to cats, is she not? I just caught Daniel Benton fondling the stable cats and saving up the fur. It's my guess he is down in the kitchens now, probably having some refreshment before Kitty's afternoon lesson.'

'Obviously, the very first attack I saw Kitty suffer was when he doctored the vinaigrette after finding it in the rose arbour . . . Every so often he must secretly top up this foul concoction. Depend upon it, for some reason of his own, he is trying to poison Kitty.'

'Poison her? Surely that cannot be?'

'Well, how else may it be explained?'

Theo and Phoebe stared at one another for a full minute before Theo strode to the door and called for a footman to summon Mr Benton to the sewing room immediately.

Theo remained standing and tapped at the top of his boot. 'You are fully recovered from your indisposition, I hope?'

Phoebe met his eyes briefly and without her usual smile. 'I was a trifle out of sorts, it was of no consequence . . . What are you going to say to Daniel?'

Theo's eyes grew cold and for a moment she had a stirring of sympathy for Daniel. 'I will ask Mr Benton what the devil he thinks he's playing at.'

* * *

The smile on Daniel Benton's face froze as he entered the room and took in the scene including the vinaigrette, emptied of its contents, standing on the desk next to Phoebe.

'Oh Lord,' he said.

'An explanation sir, if you please.' Theo's voice was icy, his lips narrowed.

Daniel Benton, whose complexion was always inclined to be pale, now looked to be queasy. 'My mother sir, her maiden name was Bellamy. My great grandfather, Matthew, was the brother of Kitty's great grandfather. I am . . . I am Kitty's cousin several times removed.'

There was a long silence. Theo's face was expressionless. 'And have you papers to prove this?'

'Yes but . . . '

'Then why this,' Theo indicated a hand to where the vinaigrette's contents were spread on the paper. 'Why not come to me with the proof? Why all this? Why cause my ward so much distress? Good God man, you could have killed her!'

Daniel put a slim fingered hand to his white brow. 'No! No, I assure you that was never the intention. At first I just wanted to see my ancestral home. I — I didn't want anything. Lord knows I'm not entitled through my mother's line, I know that. Then when I saw that Kitty had so very much and I so little, I thought that maybe if we could become friends, I could explain and she might advance me a little so — so I could start up my own music school . . . But the time to explain, never came.

'We were never alone for long enough . . . And besides — I had reason to think she would suppose my sentiments to be of a romantic nature, which I can assure you they were not and would never have been.'

'Quite,' commented Theo.

'And then,' went on Phoebe, beginning to understand. 'Last year, plans were made for Kitty to go to London and you thought you would lose your chance and that was when you realised that if you could doctor the vinaigrette and she became ill she would be returned home. And having hit on the idea, which worked so excessively well, you carried on with it.'

Phoebe's face flushed and her eyes sparkled dangerously. 'I can scarce believe you would do such a selfishly wicked thing. You have denied Kitty upwards of eighteen months of her girlhood. She's had no parties, no balls, no expeditions or beaux. No riding through the countryside, or picnics. No life as such . . .'

Two angry spots of colour appeared in Daniel's cheek and his eyes glinted with sudden indignation. 'Believe me, her life was not so very hard. She is cosseted at every turn, all her whims satisfied . . . It is amazing indeed that she is of such sweet disposition. I — I am grown very fond of her — whatever you may think . . .

'I have not had such a life. My grandfather's fortunes were not good, but he would never, never ask for assistance. But I am not too proud to ask help, not for me, but for my mother who lives in straightened circumstances in Norwich. Do you not think I have wished often that I had gone through a solicitor . . . ? But I am not used to such kind behaviour as I have been shown here and did not expect it . . . That I should not have taken advantage of it — I know full well.'

Theo was the only one in the room who remained calm. 'I think you had better go now,' he said. 'You may call tomorrow when I have informed Kitty of the situation and we will see what is to be done.'

Daniel made a stiff bow and retreated from the room.

Phoebe was left staring at Mr Prendergast. 'What will you do with him?'

Theo smiled grimly. 'I'd like to box his ears, yes, and give him a sound whipping . . . But I'm persuaded Kitty would not like that. Besides he's had a tongue lashing from you. He will lick his wounds for some time.'

Shakily, Phoebe sat down and immediately Theo came to her side. 'I had forgotten you have not been well. This morning must have been difficult to bear.' He sat beside her and tilted her face up so as to read her expression.

Phoebe struggled for composure. It was very unsettling to be scrutinised by such handsome dark eyes, so very easy to imagine tenderness in their expression. She turned her head away.

'Phoebe, what's amiss? And don't tell me 'nothing' again. I cannot endure another sleepless night worrying what I have done to displease you.'

Phoebe looked at him steadily. 'I have been thinking to return home soon. And now it seems Kitty will be better, it is time.'

A thunderous expression passed over Mr Prendergast's features. 'No. I won't allow it.'

'Pardon me, but you must. I cannot stay here any longer.'

'I don't understand. Are you really so very unhappy here? I had begun to think, to hope, that we could deal tolerably well together. Indeed I had almost persuaded myself that perhaps you even liked me a little.'

11

Phoebe could bear it no longer. 'Pray do not go on, sir,' she said. 'I have been treated with nothing but kindness and you have been above all things generous. Allowing me to ride Firefly, oh I know you made it seem like a favour you were seeking, but I'm not such a pea goose as not to know otherwise. P — please do not think I am ungrateful ... ' She broke off, finding it difficult to continue.

Mr Prendergast gazed at her steadily as she struggled for composure. 'So why can you not stay? Kitty will be quite heartbroken.'

'Please don't ask ... Please don't press me for an explanation, as I have none to give you.'

'Very well,' he sounded curt again, almost dismissive. 'It seems our country ways may be too tame for you. We lead an unexciting life, I know ... I told your brother I feared this might be the case.'

At this Phoebe looked up. 'My brother? And what may he have to do with this?'

'You must know I spoke with him on my trip from London? I put a proposition to him, which I think he looked on favourably, but I can see I was foolish to hope.'

Almost fainting, Phoebe rose to her feet. He was going to tell her of his plans to marry Kitty, possibly he would ask her to stay on a more permanent footing until he deemed Kitty old enough to be without a companion — and that she couldn't, wouldn't bear.

'Phoebe,' he put out a hand to steady her. Then the fingers that gripped her arm tightened and he turned her to face him, gave a groan and pulled her towards him.

His kiss, when it came was firm yet passionate and at first Phoebe resisted, then somehow the fight did not seem worth while and she melted against him with a feeling of desire, yet home coming that made everything right.

But it wasn't right. Even if, she admitted to herself at last, even if she had been bird-witted enough to fall in love with him — he had no business kissing her while intending to marry Kitty.

She pushed him away. 'What? What are you doing?'

Theo lifted his head. 'What I have wanted to do ever since the very first time I set eyes on you. Only of course, I didn't realise it at first.'

'Really?' said Phoebe faintly. 'But you didn't like me . . . You were always angry with me. You said I was a minx!'

Theo's expression softened. 'Well, you are,' he said, 'and a saucy one at that, but I realised when you came to Fairfield and lit up my house and my life just by your very presence, how very much you had come to mean to me. I could hardly take my eyes from you in order to be polite to my other guests.'

Phoebe was still in a state of shock. 'But Charlotte Leadbetter. Annie . . . I mean it's been whispered . . . '

'I know very well what has been whispered, but it is with no foundation. I don't enjoy her company, and she can barely tolerate my boys. Besides — she is not you.'

'But what about Kitty,' asked Phoebe. 'I thought you were saving her for yourself and you w — wanted me to look after her for you until she was old enough for marriage.'

Theo's eyebrows shot up in surprise and for a moment he held her at arms length. 'What?' he said. 'Kitty? Why on earth should I want to marry Kitty? 'Yes Mr Prendergast — No Mr Prendergast,' what a dreary life we should both have. You surely cannot have considered that seriously?'

'Oh,' said Phoebe. 'But why — why didn't you tell me before?' Her voice ended on a slight quiver.

'But,' he explained patiently, 'it wasn't until I spent that week away from you that I realised how heavy the time sat on my hands. How much I wanted to be with you, how I valued your companionship and your laughter and how very much I wanted to do this.'

His lips found hers once more and Phoebe discovered that she really had no objection to Mr Prendergast being overbearing on occasion.

'So,' he went on after a short period, 'on my way back from London, I decided to call on your brother and ask him to be discreet, as I had no confidence that you would accept my suit. He is a good fellow, your brother, over our port, he gave his word he would not tell his wife before I had spoken to you. Then when I arrived home, I found you had been out dancing with the vicar . . . I'm ashamed to say I was wildly jealous.'

'Jealous of the vicar?' Phoebe was incredulous. 'But yes, I recall you were exceedingly provoking that evening.'

'And you looked exceedingly desirable,' responded Theo. 'As you still do.'

'Oh dear . . . Beg pardon.' A flushed Kitty stood at the door. 'I will come back later.'

'No, Kitty, come in and hear Phoebe's answer for, if she will only be quiet long enough, I am about to ask her to marry me.'

Kitty's mouth curved upwards. 'Well, I should like it above all things of course, and Mrs Manningtree did say . . . ' she broke off in some confusion. 'But are you n-not too old for Phoebe? She told me once she could not abide acquainted men.'

'Oh he's excessively old and bad tempered. What's more I believe he expects me to embroider his slippers — but I shall say 'yes' in spite of all those things,' said Phoebe happily.

'Well, do please excuse me. I was only looking for my vinaigrette, but I can manage without it.'

'Yes Kitty, I'm very sure you can,' said Mr Prendergast going back to what he was doing so expertly before Kitty's interruption.

We do hope that you have enjoyed reading this large print book.

Did you know that all of our titles are available for purchase?

We publish a wide range of high quality large print books including:
Romances, Mysteries, Classics General Fiction Non Fiction and Westerns

Special interest titles available in large print are:
The Little Oxford Dictionary Music Book, Song Book Hymn Book, Service Book

Also available from us courtesy of Oxford University Press:
Young Readers' Dictionary (large print edition) Young Readers' Thesaurus (large print edition)

For further information or a free brochure, please contact us at:
Ulverscroft Large Print Books Ltd., The Green, Bradgate Road, Anstey, Leicester, LE7 7FU, England. Tel: (00 44) **0116 236 4325 Fax:** (00 44) **0116 234 0205**

FELICITY MOON

Valerie Holmes

When, in self defence, Felicity Moon strikes her employer Julian Cannon, she is forced to leave the place where her father had sent her for her own safety. Accused and jailed for bank-rolling smugglers, Squire Moon is unaware of the dangers Felicity is facing. She is given one last chance by Cannon's housekeeper in the form of a reference to Mr Lucas Packman, a man her father distrusts. Felicity faces a stark choice: trust Packman or her father.

DON'T TOUCH ME

John Russell Fearn

A jewel heist goes wrong when the escaping robbers abduct Gloria Vane, the beautiful film actress. Then as gang leader Ace Monohan falls for Gloria, it leads to dissension amongst his men, and the destruction and abandonment of his hideout. Ace, forced to go on the run, takes the stolen jewels with him. Now Gloria finds herself at the mercy of rival gangster 'Fingers' Baxter, who plans to use her to lure Ace out of hiding . . .

THE LEGACY OF THE TOWER

Sheila Lewis

Lizanne Naismith is saddened when Jeffrey Falkin, owner of her former ancestral home, Gilliestoun Tower, dies in an accident. The grief of his family turns to shock and denial when an unknown son, Alex, turns up. Lizanne is the only one to befriend him, much to the chagrin of her boyfriend Steven, Jeffrey's son. Using her skills as a researcher she investigates Alex's mysterious background. When a long-buried secret is revealed, it alters the lives of everyone involved.